TRIAL BY FIRE

A ROMANTIC SUSPENSE NOVEL

CARA C. PUTMAN

WVP

TRIAL BY FIRE

Created with Vellum

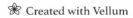

He has showed you, O man, what is good.
And what does the Lord require of you?
To act justly and to love mercy
and to walk humbly with your God.
—*Micah 6:8*

To Abigail, Jonathan, Rebecca, and Daniel. My kiddos put up with one crazy fall where this was the last of three books turned in on very tight deadlines. I enjoyed celebrating "the end" in this book by going to Madagascar 2 with you. But most of all, I am humbled that God entrusted each of you to me.

ACKNOWLEDGMENTS

Thanks to Krista Stroever and Tina Colombo. Krista, for buying this book, and Tina, for helping me make it better. Thanks to Karen Solem for constantly pushing me to slow down and find those stories that resonate.

Thanks also to Patrick Grimes, fire investigator with the Lafayette Fire Department, for his willingness to share his experience and expertise. And thanks to my colleague Greg Loyd for answering some strange and pointed questions about what he'd seen as a domestic violence prosecutor that complicated cases, which helped me make Tricia's life miserable.

1

Thursday, *Lincoln, Nebraska*

Another broken dream rested in front of Deputy County Attorney Tricia Jamison.

The phone ringing on the desk pulled her thoughts from the file. She glanced at her watch. The afternoon had evaporated while she flipped through new case files and absorbed the dashed hopes each one represented. She'd taken the job because she wanted to help people, those who didn't have anyone to protect them. Each time she got a new file, she had the opportunity to make a difference for a family. She'd seen God heal families when directed to the right resources. But every time another domestic violence case crossed her desk it was hard not to grow discouraged. Too many times the hope of happily-ever-afters had gone horribly wrong. She shook her head and grabbed the still ringing phone.

"Tricia Jamison, deputy prosecutor."

"Trish, this is Caleb. There's a fire at Mom's." Her brother's voice had an edge of tension she hadn't heard in a while. As a police investigator, he usually kept his emotions tightly controlled. She hadn't heard him sound so rattled since last year when a stalker set his sights on Caleb's girlfriend, Dani Richard. Her breath caught in her chest as she shut the file on her desk. "How bad?"

"Don't know. I heard it on my scanner before Mom called."

"Is she safe?"

There was a pause, then a sigh. "Yes."

"I'm leaving now." Her jaw clenched. Images of flames lapping at her mother's home raced through her mind. The home encapsulated so many memories, both good and bad.

Tricia grabbed her purse and keys, and ran toward the elevator. She slid to a stop at her paralegal's desk. "Family emergency. I'll be back tomorrow."

"I'll cover for you." The woman leaned back in her chair, a concerned expression on her face.

"Thanks." Tricia jogged the rest of the way to the elevator. She punched the down button and paced until the doors opened.

Twenty minutes later she'd crossed town and pulled into her mom's neighborhood. Flashing lights drew her toward the small ranch home. She parked several houses down, and rushed to join Caleb and Mom in the neighbor's yard. Caleb had his arm around their mother's shoulders, and she'd sunk against his side, an unusual posture for one who liked to stand firmly on her own two feet. The heavy smell of smoke curled through the air, but no matter how Tricia squinted against the western sun, the house looked intact. In fact, there weren't many firefighters in the front yard.

"Are you okay?"

The petite woman tipped her chin up, brown eyes flashing. "Of course. Some kid decided the garage made a good fire-starter."

"Where's Frank?" Tricia's stepfather usually rushed to his wife's side anytime she whimpered or looked a little cross. Tricia couldn't fault his devotion to her mom.

"At work. He wanted to come home, but I told him not to hurry. It's a small fire." A tremble in Mom's voice belied her strong front.

"From Caleb's call I thought the flames had engulfed the house."

Mom poked him in the ribs. "I told you not to make a big deal."

"A fire is never small." He rubbed his side with a frown. "The wind blows in the wrong direction, and the outcome could change. It almost reached the house."

"But it didn't. Relax." There was still a tightness at the corner of her eyes even as Mom forced a smile.

"Sure." Caleb grimaced over her head at Tricia. "We'll never worry about you when panic fills your voice. Fires are everyday occurrences."

"You can't protect everyone." Even as she said the words, Tricia knew he wouldn't accept them.

"You believe that?" He rolled his eyes. "Sure. That's why you're a prosecutor."

"Someone has to do it." Tricia grinned at him. She'd had a lifetime to perfect the art of poking his weak spots. Tell Caleb he couldn't take care of everyone, and he bristled like a porcupine. Good thing she was a pro at sidestepping his quills.

"All right, you two. You can bicker all you want inside. I want to get out of this yard before we trample the Johnsons' grass. You know how fastidious George is." Mom tugged Caleb's sleeve until he joined her.

A couple of firefighters turned the corner from the backyard into the front. One pulled off his helmet and ran a hand through smooshed hair, sweat streaking his face. He caught Tricia's glance and grimaced. Her heart stopped, and she took a shuddering breath. Noah Brust. In the flesh, and looking even better in his turnout coat with soot on his face than he had the last time she'd seen him in the courtroom.

"Mrs. Randol?" His voice was low, with a rich timbre to it. It tickled her senses, and her stomach tightened, even though the man ignored her.

"Yes," her mother answered.

"I'm Noah Brust with the Lincoln Fire Department. We've contained the fire. The shed will be a total loss, but we kept it from the house."

Mom put a trembling hand to her mouth, then nodded. "Thank you. We'll replace the things in the shed. Frank will probably enjoy the excuse to buy more tools."

"Investigator Caleb Jamison, LPD." Caleb extended his hand, and the firefighter shook it. "This is my sister, Tricia Jamison."

Noah turned a blank expression her way. "We've met."

Tricia nodded, searching for a hint of emotion on his face. Even anger seemed better than the nothingness he registered when looking at her. Instead, he wore a look of schooled indifference. This from the rugged fireman who'd almost swept her off her feet when she'd prepped him for his testimony during the Lincoln Life fire trial a year before. Despite the attraction that zinged between them, he'd made it clear at the close of his testimony that he wanted nothing to do with her.

She stifled the urge to grab his collar and force him to acknowledge her. Mom threw her a questioning look, and Tricia shook her head. Now was not the time to explain.

"Any clues on how the fire started?" Caleb pulled her attention back to the fire.

Noah focused on Caleb. "The captain will likely call in the fire investigation team. Until they work their magic I can guess at a cause, but that's it. We'll keep an eye on the fire while we clean up. We'll leave only when we're sure the fire's out, but it's safe to go inside your home now."

"Thank you." Mom pulled the collar of her jacket tight around her throat against the October wind as she hurried toward the house.

Heat climbed Tricia's face, and she turned to find Noah watching her. "Thanks for helping Mom."

"You're welcome."

She fought the urge to rub her arms, try to generate some warmth against the chill emanating from him. "You're still angry about the Lincoln Life case? I did everything the law allowed."

His blue eyes, which had so captured her attention before, had frosted over. Noah snorted and shook his head. "Thanks to you, I read a dozen articles accusing my father—one of the best firefighters I've ever known—of negligence in his duties." His voice rose with each word. "He died a hero, but you didn't raise a finger to stop them from slandering him at the trial."

She looked around for a way to escape the barrage of angry words. "I'm sorry you don't appreciate the rules of court and their limitations. And don't forget, we won." Tricia turned at the sound of more cars pulling into the cul-de-sac. The Channel 13 Jeep jerked into park as Caleb reappeared at her shoulder.

"You okay, sis?" Caleb furrowed his brow until the eyebrows merged.

"Fine. I'll be there in a minute, Caleb." She turned to Firefighter Brust and twisted her lips into what she hoped passed for a smile. "I'm sorry I couldn't do more to protect you and your father. Now, if you don't want to create another scene worthy of the papers, let me pass. The media have arrived." She tipped her chin, pushed past him and marched to Caleb's side. "Let's go inside now, please."

Tricia refused to look back as Caleb hurried her into the house. She tried to ignore the tremble in her limbs when she sat on the couch next to her mother.

"Anything you need to tell me?" Caleb stood in front of her in full big brother mode.

"An unpleasant reminder of a case from last year."

"Looked like more."

"No." Tricia shook her head. "He thinks I didn't do my job. There's nothing I can do to change his mind. If I'm lucky, I won't run into him again."

Today had been a fluke. That's all.

Then why did the pain hiding in his cold eyes cut so?

~

NOAH WATCHED the media park on the cul-de-sac. He stood straight and prepared for the onslaught. "The vultures descend."

Graham Jackson groaned and yanked his helmet off. "Come on, man. Hold it together."

"You're right." Noah frowned and ran a hand over his face. Some days he felt so tired, he wondered how long he'd keep up with the job. Fighting through the lingering impact of the knee he'd injured in the Lincoln Life fire seemed impossible. He tried to hide it on the job, but rarely succeeded. "So, I lost my composure."

"Yep." Graham climbed onto the fire truck, tossing his helmet onto the seat next to him. He grabbed two bottles of water and tossed one to Noah. "Fortunately, the press arrived late and didn't see your show. What was that all about, anyway? I've never seen you that worked up around a woman." Noah unscrewed the lid and sat opposite Graham. He forced the image of Tricia's face from his mind. She looked as beautiful as she had when he'd met her the year before. He'd been instantly smitten with the spunky lawyer...but couldn't let himself think about that now. Not after the way she'd let him down. "Hope you're right about the media." He swiped the cool bottle against his forehead, ignoring Graham's stare. "I keep waiting for it to get easier. You'd think it would after a year."

"You still haven't answered my question."

"She was the attorney on the Lincoln Life case."

Graham looked toward the house. "She's cute."

"I'd hoped she was more." Much more. "But I was wrong."

"Don't push so hard. This was a simple outbuilding fire, and you barked orders like flames were engulfing the Cornhusker Hotel."

"I acted crazy. She brings that out in me." Noah ran his fingers through his hair and grimaced.

"No. A little overzealous, but it's okay. Temper it. That's all I'm saying."

An hour later, the firefighters cleared the scene and headed back to the fire station. The rest of the shift dragged as Noah tried to focus on the paperwork in front of him, rather than Tricia Jamison.

That night, long after he should have been asleep, Noah lay in bed and couldn't stop thinking about the prosecutor and the trial. Before he'd taken the stand, he'd had a dinner invitation planned for Tricia. Test the sparks between them. Then she'd let him down during what she'd said would be an easy cross-examination. He forced the memory from his mind, but thoughts of his father's death marched into its place.

His chest tightened at the flashback of how close he'd gotten to saving his father, but not close enough. When the ceiling collapsed between them, he'd known he'd failed. Waited too long. Tried too hard to save everybody else. Failed to save his father's life.

Thanks to Tricia Jamison, he hadn't salvaged the man's reputation, either. That he couldn't forgive. No matter how beautiful she looked.

2

Friday

The next morning Barry Williams, the company officer, called Noah into his office. “Rumor has it you’re interested in learning fire investigation.”

Noah stood straighter. “Yes, sir.”

“Think you’ll have time?” Williams rocked back in his chair as he stroked his mustache. It looked more like a hairy caterpillar than a true mustache, but to each his own.

“Yes. I’d welcome the challenge, sir.” With his knee, he might need options. The thought galled him, but investigations might fill the void.

“Thought so. We’ve decided to start you with Investigator Brian Weary.” Noah nodded and turned to leave, trying to hide the excitement inside him. “And, Brust...”

He turned back around. “Yes?”

“Remember, you asked for this assignment. Weary isn’t the easiest man to deal with.”

“I’ll keep that in mind.” Weary’s irascible reputation preceded him, but Noah could handle it.

Noah closed the office door behind him and returned to the

holding area where several firefighters were killing time watching TV. He sank onto an empty folding chair next to the couch.

"Brust." An angry voice yelled from behind him.

Noah turned to identify the speaker.

"Looks like your education is about to start." Graham gestured to the doorway.

Noah stood and joined Weary in the doorway. "Noah Brust, sir."

"I know who you are. So you think you're ready to come off the truck?" The stocky, intense man stared at Noah. "I guess we'll see. We've got a ton of work to do before the scene gets contaminated. I've been through it once, but there's more to do. You'll have to keep up."

"I can do that."

Weary snorted. "That's what they all say. We'll see if you can." Noah began to reply, but Weary kept talking. "I understand you worked this fire."

Noah froze. "The Randol fire?"

"That's right." Weary's stare challenged Noah. "Is that a problem?"

"N-no, sir." Not a problem at all...except he'd land squarely in the path of the woman he'd spent half the night trying to force from his mind. Surely, God wouldn't want him to spend time with her.

He turned to leave the room, and his knee locked in place. He grimaced, grateful that Weary had already stalked down the hallway and couldn't see his face. What had he gotten himself into?

~

TRICIA'S STEPS dragged as she stepped off the elevator and headed to her office in the City-County Building. After running out the previous day, she'd have piled up phone messages and e-mails, but she couldn't motivate herself to get started. Noah Brust's hurt look kept invading her mind.

How could ten minutes of interaction resurrect the pain where he was concerned? After working with him during trial prep, she'd felt certain he was interested in her. When the mere sight of him sent her pulse racing, she couldn't hide her own attraction. Noah was strong, almost intimidating, yet a hint of compassion peeked through as they talked.

He'd appeared so different from most men she knew. Maybe even on caliber with her big brother Caleb.

Then the trial had ended, and he'd squashed any hope of exploring the future together.

No, he'd handed her head to her as he stormed from the courtroom. She hadn't heard from him since. Hadn't even run into the man until the fire yesterday.

With all the firefighters in the city, why did he have to respond to Mom's fire?

Tricia tossed her purse in a desk drawer and her briefcase on the floor. The chair groaned as she sank onto it. She looked at her desk for inspiration or a distraction. Yesterday's newspaper lay open near the top. Tricia pulled it out and scanned the pages. She slowed when she reached the obituaries, praying she wouldn't see a notice for one of her former clients. None of the names looked familiar until she reached the bottom of the page. Timothy Gillmore. He'd been six. No one should die that young.

Something bothered her about his name. Why did it tickle her memory? She skimmed the obituary and realized why it seemed familiar. The boy had been critically injured in the Lincoln Life blaze. After the firefighters pulled him from the debris in the building, he'd been medevacked to Creighton University Medical Center in Omaha, but had never awakened from his coma. Hadn't his family joined the lawsuit against the city and the fire department? Her thoughts spiraled back to the events she'd spent most of the previous night trying to forget.

The Lincoln Life case had been an anomaly. But she'd empathized with the firefighter's defense. She'd even been cautiously happy to spend time with Noah Brust. A step outside her routine cases. She'd done the assigned job. Helped with her piece of the defense and won the case for the city. She knew she couldn't make everybody happy all the time, no matter how hard she tried. But it didn't make it easier when confronted with someone who felt wronged by her actions. Or in this case inaction.

The pain in his eyes when he'd looked at her yesterday— she couldn't shake it.

Tricia folded the paper and placed it to the side. The stack of files beckoned her. Time to buckle down and prepare for the Parker trial. The trial started in one week. If she didn't at least review the file and line up witnesses, she'd regret it later.

The stack of files appeared to sway as Tricia eyed it. She grabbed the top file. Pulled out the first document—a photo— and flipped it over. Linda Parker, the battered wife who'd filed the charges.

"Knock, knock."

Tricia looked up to find deputy prosecutor and lunch buddy Sydney Sims standing in the doorway. The brunette looked polished in a designer suit and heels.

"Hey."

"Another case getting to you?" Sydney sank into the chair opposite Tricia's desk.

"Yes. This one more so than others." For reasons Tricia would never explain, not even to Sydney.

"These cases take so much from you. Have you considered reassignment?"

"No. I can make a difference for the victims." She had seen it, time and again.

"Then ask Charlie to reassign this case. It can't be worth the toll."

If only Sydney understood how great the burden truly was.

Sydney leaned forward, concern on her face. "Why does this case bother you so much? You've worked these cases long enough to not let them get to you."

"Let's just say it hits close to home." Tricia rubbed her face. "I hate seeing what men will do to their wives. At least Parker didn't beat his kids."

"You can't save them all, Tricia. The victims have to want help."

"This one does." Tricia would work past her own history with Parker to provide that help.

Sydney's cell phone rang. She looked at the number and frowned. "I've got to take this. Let me know if you want or need to talk more about this one."

Tricia nodded, then turned back to the file. Linda Parker's photo stared at her. Blood discolored her face under her nose, and bruises already formed under her eyes. Tricia felt bile rise at the images the photo brought back to mind.

She hurried to close the file.

How could she objectively prosecute Andrew Parker, the man who seemed too good to be true when he'd dated Tricia in college? How true that had turned out to be. She fingered the scar on her jaw. While makeup covered the line, the remnants of that attack still scarred her heart. Would that damage ever fade? Could she trust another man? And would she be able to project the image of a detached, yet passionate prosecutor without allowing the fear and guilt that had kept her from filing charges against Parker to overwhelm her?

A niggle at the back of her mind made her wonder...again... should she tell her boss about her history with the man? No, not if she wanted this to be the catharsis that finally ended the lingering effects of her nightmare.

She didn't really have a choice. She had to either force herself to ignore her pain, or ask the county attorney to reassign the case, something he wouldn't do without an explanation. She couldn't tell Charlie anything about her past with Andrew. Open that door, and it would be too hard to close.

Tricia returned her focus to the case files, determined to ignore the memories that seared her mind. Andrew could not hurt her anymore. And neither could any other man. She'd kept them at a distance for years. That wouldn't change now.

BRIAN WEARY SAT behind his desk, fingers steepled under his chin as he droned on. Noah took a deep breath. *Lord, help me make the most of this opportunity without throttling the guy.*

In two short hours, Weary had earned his reputation. His didactic tone made Noah want to run from the room. He stayed from a deep desire to learn how to read a fire.

"Let's see this fire." Weary launched from his chair and marched toward his car without waiting to see if Noah followed. "You were there."

Noah hesitated. Should he respond? The silence stretched, and Noah rushed to fill it. "Yes, sir. The dispatcher assigned the call to us. We arrived..."

"I don't need an oral report."

Okey-dokey. Speak when spoken to, but not if an answer isn't required. Noah scratched his head and climbed into the passenger seat. This might be harder than he thought. Maybe he should've been content with his regular duties. No, he needed the bigger challenge and the security it provided if his knee couldn't keep up with the fires.

Weary whipped his '67 Mustang through traffic as if he were driving in the Indy 500. Noah resisted the urge to grab onto anything mounted to the car that would stabilize him. He let out his breath when Weary turned into the residential area and found his way to the site. Thirty-five miles per hour had never felt so wonderful. Weary pulled the car to the curb and grabbed a toolbox from the backseat.

"Show me the site of this conflagration."

"I'd call it more of a bonfire. The shed provided the wood instead of logs." Noah stumbled to a stop when Weary eyed him, bushy eyebrows arched. "It's this way, sir."

Even if Noah hadn't seen the fire firsthand, the smell of smoke lingered in the air, providing a trail to the smoldering ashes. He stood back as Weary walked around the remains. "What makes you think someone started this fire?"

Noah moved closer to the remnant of the shed and pointed to a corner charred darker than the others. "The discoloration there indicates an accelerant helped the fire along. Electricity doesn't pipe into the shed, so it couldn't be a short. Skies remained clear yesterday, so lightning wasn't the culprit." He shrugged and pushed his hands in his pockets. "Everything points to someone starting the fire."

Weary walked around the site again, head cocked at an angle. He crouched down and pulled on gloves. Opening his case, he pulled out a probe and poked around the ashes. "What color were the flames?"

Closing his eyes, Noah tried to remember the scene when the truck first arrived. The controlled chaos of unrolling the hose and hooking up to the fire hydrant dominated the mental image. By the time he reached the shed, his colleagues had aimed the water at the fire and the flames had eased. "I didn't see them before water soaked the area."

The sound of a car pulling into the driveway caused Noah to turn around. Tricia's overprotective brother strode through the yard toward them.

"Hello." Jamison stuck his hand out. Noah grasped it, while Weary ignored them. "Find anything?"

"We haven't been here long." Noah glanced at Weary digging through the ashes. "Investigator Brian Weary with the fire investigation team is the man hunched on the ground."

Weary looked up long enough to nod with a frown. "Who are you, and what are you doing at my scene?"

"Investigator Caleb Jamison, LPD. This is my mother's house." He stood his ground. "What's the cause?"

Weary's teeth ground so hard Noah heard them. "You can wait for my report along with everyone else."

Caleb shook his head. "Sorry, but I work homicides. If someone set this fire, I need to know, so I can track down suspects. Yesterday. Before anything else happens."

"You've made a dangerous assumption, kid. You're an investigator? Then you should know the importance of keeping an open mind."

Noah wouldn't wager on who would hold out longest. Both men looked entirely too used to getting their way. He choked down a chuckle. Someone would lose this time. Noah took a step back. He didn't want to be collateral damage caught in the crossfire. Good thing he kept his ego in line. Most of the time.

Caleb tightened his stance and stared at Weary. "Is he always this arrogant, Brust?"

"That's the rumor." Noah shot a glance at Weary. Maybe honesty wasn't the best policy right now.

"As long as my family is involved, I'll follow this investigation. Nothing happens to them on my watch."

Caleb's tone of voice sounded defensive. His reaction seemed to extend beyond taking care of his own. "I'll keep you updated," Noah said.

With a nod, Caleb spun on his heel and stalked out of the yard. At the fence, he paused, then returned. "Brust?"

"Yeah?"

"Here's my contact info. Give me a call when you have a moment." He held out his business card. Challenge filled his eyes, this time directed squarely at Noah.

Noah nodded in one quick motion, taking the card from his hand. Jamison left Noah rubbing the back of his neck.

"Whenever you're done staring after the LPD, I could use your help."

Noah moved back to the shed and crouched beside Weary. "What's up?"

"See this line here? There's extra charring in the wood. This is the line of accelerant. Go get the buckets from my trunk. It's time to clear back the debris."

Noah nodded, and didn't bother pointing out that he'd said exactly the same thing about the accelerant a few minutes ago. "Thoughts on the accelerant?"

"My guess is plain old gasoline. We'll take debris back to the lab for tests, but if it's gas, there won't be much to trace and it'll take weeks to get the results." Weary rubbed a hand across his cheek, leaving a streak of soot. Weary gestured toward his kit. "Grab the buckets. Time to put you to work."

The afternoon flew by in a flurry of following Weary's garbled instructions, and then rushing back to the fire station for his regular shift. Fortunately, there were no callouts to fires. Even so, the smell of smoke saturated him after the time at the scene. Usually such a day would leave Noah bored, but when he drove home after dinner, he was grateful for the chance to catch his breath.

He entered his ground-floor apartment and kicked the stack of mail away from the slot in the door. Jessie, his two-year-old golden retriever mix, tore around the corner, feet sliding on the linoleum. "Hey, girl. Ready for some exercise?"

Fifteen minutes later, Noah had changed and was taking a casual jog. He gritted his teeth against the pain that pulsed through his knee. He had to push past this or he'd never get back to top form. The pain made a good distraction from the day, and Tricia Jamison. Jessie pulled him through the neighborhood, wanting a faster pace, and Noah tried to keep up as he put the day behind him. Tomorrow would be better. He had a date. One Graham had set up. Hopefully, this one would be an improvement over the last debacle. As soon as he and Jessie reentered the apartment, the phone rang as he flipped through his mail.

"Hello?"

"I'm looking for Noah Brust."

"You've got him." The voice tickled a corner of his memory.

"Okay." A long pause stretched as he waited for the woman to speak.

"Look, can I help you?"

An expulsion of air rushed through the phone. "I hope so. This is Tricia Jamison. I'd like an update. Caleb said you hadn't called yet."

Tricia Jamison. So much for not thinking about her again tonight. How could he feel a pull to her from a few words? A flash of something unsettling followed the thought. He growled in the confusion. "What is it with you and your brother wanting answers? It'll take a while. How did you get my home number?"

"You're on White Pages." Defensiveness laced her voice, but the words stopped abruptly. "I'm sorry. I really wanted to make sure you won't let our past interfere with your investigation."

Our past? She said it like something had actually developed between them. Something more than the figments of his imagination. "I wouldn't let that happen."

"Truly?"

He took a deep breath. Why did she push so hard? "Yes. I know it's hard to worry about someone you love. I promise, as soon as there's information, I'll get it to your mother."

"All right." A hitch in her voice communicated how important this must be to her. "I need to know she'll be okay."

"There's no reason to worry." He looked at his watch and slid down the hall to his bedroom. "Anything else?"

"I guess not."

"Great." He kicked off his shoes. Time to end this conversation. "Next time call the fire department."

A huff of air sounded. "Don't worry. I won't bother you with questions again." She hung up before he could respond.

He stared at the phone, tempted to call her back and apologize. He'd been rude, which wasn't like him at all. She was right—he'd just let their past influence his behavior. But the thought of admitting it made his stomach turn. Besides, did it matter if she thought him rude? It wouldn't bother her for long. He remembered how she'd been at the trial—so confident and self-assured. She hadn't cared about what he'd thought or said back then. If she had, she wouldn't have let him down.

Nope, he didn't need to call her back. He needed to plan tomorrow night's date. If he concentrated on that, maybe he'd forget the hot-tempered attorney with beautiful doe eyes and a great smile.

3

Saturday

Tricia parked in front of the Green Gateau on the edge of the Haymarket area and collected her thoughts. The day had lagged, not helped at all when Mom had called to remind her that today was their weekly tea and dessert. Tricia loved her mom and the charming, red brick restaurant with its black wrought iron fence, street lamps, and red and green umbrellas shading outdoor seating, but exhaustion weighed her down. She couldn't pretend to have the energy to enjoy the company or the treat.

She stared at the ivy crawling up the brick edge of the building and steadied her breathing. The cafe was one of her favorite spots, with its stained-glass window embedded in the ceiling and the antiques, lending an old-world feel to the place. If only the conversation could match the ambience. Some hitch in her mom's voice had a knot tightening in Tricia's stomach. The tension wouldn't ease no matter how often she breathed slowly or told herself she was once again over-thinking a nuance she might not have heard.

A car door slammed and Tricia looked up. Mom hustled toward the door dressed in a denim skirt and bulky turtleneck. Tricia should stop her, let her know she hadn't made it inside the restaurant, but she didn't.

Father, help me.

With the Parker trial barreling down on her, each day made it harder to maintain the cheerful mask. The one she'd perfected over the years to hide the pain and roiling emotions. Mom couldn't see the way she really felt—not today. Mom had pushed her toward Andrew and told Tricia they were a great match. She'd chosen to ignore the aggression and violence that shimmered under the surface. Tricia shouldn't be surprised, since her mother had never noticed those traits in Frank, either.

Someday she had to repair her relationship with her mother. It would be so much easier if Frank weren't around. How could Mom remain so oblivious to the tension and love a monster? Tricia's face pinched, and her scar warmed. Maybe if Frank hadn't sauntered into her bedroom one too many times, she wouldn't have run to Andrew Parker.

Tricia squared her shoulders. Somehow she'd hold on to her happy mask. She deflated at the thought that Mom didn't care enough to notice the facade.

Tricia stepped from her Miata and pulled her jacket closer. A nip teased the air as it swirled around her. She crunched through dry leaves dusting the sidewalk, feeling as fragile as the dried remnants. Ready or not, fall colored the landscape.

Enough stalling.

A sweet aroma filled her senses as she entered the restaurant and passed the pastry case. She followed the hostess to a table tucked in one of the restaurant's many nooks. Mom looked beautiful, with the rust-colored turtleneck highlighting her placid face. She turned her face, tilting it up to accept Tricia's kiss.

"You look nice today." Mom's voice carried a lilt.

"Thanks." She grabbed the menu before she had to say anything else, grateful for the wail of a saxophone in the background that caught her mom's attention.

Mom winced. "That note was a bit off." She shook her head as if to clear the lingering sound from her mind. "What tickles your taste buds today?"

"The cream scone with lemon curd and a cup of espresso." A sure recipe to charge Tricia up on sugar and caffeine to survive the hour.

The waitress placed a glass of iced tea in front of Mom and took their orders.

After she left, Tricia searched for words to start the conversation. She hadn't been tongue-tied around Mom until Daddy died. Then Frank came, and the nightmare started.

"I'm so glad you could join me for tea today, Tricia." Mom smiled, the one that made her whole face light up. "Frank's fifty-fifth birthday is coming up in a few weeks. I thought we should throw a party for him, and you could help me plan it."

Tricia stared at her mother. A party for Frank? "What?"

"Plan a party. Streamers. Cake. Singing. I thought we could get some of his buddies together, Caleb can grill and we'll have the obligatory cake."

"I can't do that." It felt as if the dentist had suctioned her mouth dry. Celebrate the man who had molested her?

"Why not?"

"Mom..." Tricia tried to hold back the words. Now wasn't the time to bring everything out in the open. She'd held it in for years—why not keep doing that? "I've got an intense trial coming up at work. I'm focusing all my time on preparing for it."

The waitress approached the table with a tray laden with her drink and the desserts. "Here you go, ladies. Need anything else?"

Tricia tried to smile her thanks, then took a sip of the rich espresso. *God, show me what to do. I want to move past this pain that has me trapped in the past.*

"I don't understand why you're always too busy to help when it comes to Frank." Mom doctored her tea with two packets of sweetener. "Don't worry about the party. Maybe I should make it for us old folks anyway." Mom dabbed at her lips with her linen napkin. "Did your week wrap up well?"

"Yes. Fairly routine things. In and out of court." Tricia cleared her throat. "Everything back to normal with the shed?"

"Yes." Mom placed her elbows on the tabletop and leaned toward her. "What went on with the firefighter and you? How do you know each other?"

So Mom wanted the background. Tricia rolled her eyes, then froze when Mom frowned at her. Tricia sipped her espresso, relishing the bracing richness. "The Lincoln Life case last year. He testified for the fire department and thinks I set him up during the trial."

Mom puckered her lips. "So long ago. I doubt he remembers." She waved her hand in the air as if brushing away a pesky thought. "Don't you think it's time you got out? You're always using work or something else as an excuse to hide in your house on the weekends."

"That's not true. I spend a lot of time with the singles group from church."

"When a trial doesn't keep you working all hours of the day and night."

"It's my job." Tricia resisted the urge to pout.

"And in ten years you'll wish you'd rearranged your priorities."

The hostess showed a young family to a table near theirs. The husband and wife held hands, even as he carried a baby carrier with a baby decked out in pink from head to toe. The image could have come from the dream she'd buried in her heart. A husband who adored her and treated her like a treasure, who could see beyond her past and its pain to the promise of a future. A baby who shared the best of both of them, and served as a reminder that the future could always be a fresh start.

Tricia pressed against her eyes, before the tears could escape. She wanted the dream, but her work—and her past—showed how quickly dreams turned to nightmares. Mom tapped her manicured nails against the table, pulling Tricia back to their conversation. "Which one of your friends is going to be a grandmother now?"

Mom waved a hand in the air as if batting the accusation to the side. "Come on."

"Mother."

"Oh, all right. Betty Haines. Her daughter is pregnant with Betty's third granddaughter. And she's younger than you. Your biological clock is ticking."

As if that proved a point. "You're more concerned that you won't have grandchildren. Go talk to Caleb and Dani."

Her mom sighed dramatically. "Test the waters. That's all I ask. There are men out there. Someone like that firefighter, without the history."

A strangled sound came from the table behind Tricia's left shoulder. A startled look covered her mother's face. Tricia turned to look and immediately wished she hadn't. Noah Brust's ruggedly handsome face stared at her, jaw squared, eyes flashing or dancing. She couldn't tell which. A woman sat next to him, lithe form so close she might as well be sitting on him.

"Mrs. Randol. Tricia." Noah's voice sounded deliberately casual as he said her name.

Tricia tried to ignore the flash of discomfort. What had he heard? Her mind reviewed the conversation as heat climbed her neck. This on top of their earlier conversation? She longed to disappear.

"Noah." The woman next to him whined. She didn't like his focus off her.

Noah forced a smile at Tricia. "A pleasure, ladies." He swiveled back toward the model seated next to him.

Tricia eased back around and faced her mother.

Tricia shrugged off the brief exchange. It shouldn't make the scarf at her neck feel so tight. Why did it matter what he thought of her?

~

THE WOMAN next to Noah blathered on about nothing. Graham had set him up with the promise that Lisle would wow him. Not so much. He'd have to call this a swing and a miss. Almost from the moment Noah picked her up, he'd known exactly how the evening would go. Not fast enough.

Graham was right on one point—Lisle was a looker. But every

word out of her mouth centered on herself. Who found such self-centered conversation appealing? This would be the last time he let Graham suggest the perfect woman for him.

Lisle pulled on his sleeve, a pout marring her apple red lips. “Where did you go?”

Did she really expect him to tell her his thoughts? On a first date? Redirection it was then. “What brought you to Lincoln?” He picked at the crumbs on his plate.

She started talking again, seemingly mollified, and Noah glanced at his watch. If things went smoothly, he would drop her off at her apartment in an hour. There must be a lesson buried in this endless, waste-of-time evening. A reason why the only thing to catch and hold his attention was the jolt of electricity he’d felt when he realized Tricia Jamison was in the same room. He’d noticed her the moment she strode into the restaurant, looking as if she was about to head into battle. Something made her feel the need to take charge, yet she’d floundered for words during her conversation with her mother. He’d never seen her like that.

No, the Tricia he knew from a year ago would impress anyone. Poised, with every hair perfectly in place. And a mind that kept her words sharply on target.

“You did it again.” Indignation painted a mask on Lisle’s face.

“Did what?”

“Disappeared.” Lisle crossed her arms and leaned away from him. “If I’m uninteresting, you should take me home. Now.”

Noah felt a twinge of remorse. Maybe Lisle wasn’t his type, but still his mama had raised him to show better manners than ignoring his date. “Are you sure?”

“Yes.”

Noah waved the waitress over and settled the check. He left the tip on the table and helped Lisle into her jacket.

As they left his gaze settled on Tricia. There was a tension in the way she sat that he’d never noticed, not even during the trial. Then she’d held herself erect out of engagement. Here she’d steeled herself against some type of assault. As if she feared what might come next.

Could she be afraid of him?

The thought made him stumble and his stomach clenched against the meal he'd just eaten.

Their interactions played through his mind. He'd been hard on her the last few times they'd spoken. Maybe harder than he'd intended or the situation warranted. Had she been hurt by his actions and words? Tricia was strong, always in control. If she were as on top of things as she'd seemed, why couldn't she have protected him at the trial? That was the root of his anger, but now he started to wonder. Had he expected too much from her? Been unrealistic?

Was he part of the reason sadness shaded her eyes?

He helped Lisle into his truck, and rubbed his neck as he walked around to the driver's side, trying to focus on her rather than Tricia. Lisle didn't make it easy, though. If she couldn't find a mute switch, he'd have a full-blown headache before he dropped her off. Graham owed him. This evening was exhibit one for another reason not to date. It never worked for him.

Once he got home, Noah tossed his keys on a table. Maybe the way to get Tricia out of his mind was to figure out what had happened at her mom's. Then he could move on and forget about her again. He'd done it once. It shouldn't be harder the second time.

4

Sunday

"You know this wasn't some dumb kid trying to see what could burn." Tricia didn't even try to hide her exasperation as the family sat around Mom's table for Sunday dinner. Mom and Frank should know better, even if her mom did like to ignore anything that could turn unpleasant. Why didn't Caleb jump in? He was a police investigator, after all.

"Tricia, let's not argue." Mom pushed her hair behind her ears, then picked up her fork.

Frank wiped his mouth. "Your mom worked hard to make this nice meal for you."

Tricia bit the inside of her mouth to keep from screaming. They shouldn't treat this like every other after-church dinner. Someone had torched her mom's shed, and she wouldn't let it go. "Caleb, you agree with me, don't you?"

"Yes." Caleb's eyebrows knitted together. "Right now, I think it's one of the guys I investigated rather than some bored kid." He leaned his elbows on the table and stared at Mom. 'There are dangerous men on that list."

"I really think the two of you are worked up over nothing." She looked at Frank, who seemed intent on ignoring the topic. Tricia wanted to shake him and make Mom listen. While Mom's voice stayed soft and undaunted, it marginalized Tricia's fears.

Tricia put her head in her hands. "You aren't listening."

Frank chuckled. "I thought you said the kids were grown, Allison. Not sure I'd have married you if I'd known they'd stay so melodramatic into adulthood."

Tricia gritted her teeth as she settled back in her seat with a placid expression painted on her face. Frank sat there sounding so superior, as usual. He seemed to know what to do to make her feel weak and overemotional. She rubbed at the headache forming at her temples. One big, happy family. Yep, that's what they had. What she wouldn't give to be back at the office working on someone else's mess. Anything would be better than being stuck at another family dinner, pretending.

"Kids, enough. This is my house. No one was injured. Frank even gets to shop for more tools. It's done." She picked up her fork and pointed at the chocolate decadence on her plate. "I'm not letting this cake go to waste."

Caleb's jaw dropped, and Tricia assumed that her face matched his. It didn't matter who started the fire? Good thing the cake lived up to its name or she might have to leave right then. Mom loved to bury her head in the sand, but surely she had to recognize this was serious.

Caleb took a breath, and Tricia imagined him counting to ten. "We'll talk later."

In no time the conversation turned to which team would win the afternoon football game. Tricia tuned them out. She might be a Nebraskan, but today she couldn't bring herself to care about professional football. Instead, she found herself wishing there was someone in her life who would really hear her concerns—listen to *her* and pay attention to her feelings.

Maybe a man like Noah Brust. Her thoughts stilled. Why on earth would she think of him? He clearly hated her. She wished the thought didn't leave a stone of regret in her stomach.

The conversation spun around Tricia. She'd rather escape to her home and curl up on the couch with a mug of tea and the latest bestseller. Avoid the pile of work she'd dragged home in her briefcase.

"Are you going to eat the cake or poke it to death?" Frank's gravelly voice pulled her from her thoughts.

"I'm finished." Tricia pushed back from the table and grabbed her plate. "I'll get started in the kitchen, Mom." She walked away before her mom could voice the question plastered on her face. Someday she needed to stop hiding. But not yet. She couldn't force the secrets into the light.

Tricia kept Mom talking while they cleaned the lunch dishes. "I'm headed home. Relax a bit before the crazy week starts."

Mom's brow wrinkled, and concern filled her eyes. "Everything all right?"

"Sure. Just stay alert, okay? Don't want you here if whoever started the fire comes back."

"Pshaw." Mom waved a hand in the air. "It won't happen. Even if it did, Frank's here to take care of me. He's a good man, Tricia. You know that."

Tricia resisted the urge to roll her eyes. "Sure, Mom." She kissed her cheek. "See you later."

The sound of the TV blared from the family room. Frank's TV filled one of the small walls. Tricia peeked in and saw Frank and Caleb jumping like kids at a trampoline park. With a shake of her head, she continued down the hall and slipped out. A well of loneliness swelled as she drove home. Her small cottage on the tree lined street in an older neighborhood felt empty and forlorn instead of homey. Should she find a roommate? When she'd wrestled with loneliness before, she'd considered it, but always abandoned the idea. She didn't want to fight over whose turn it was to buy milk or who needed to clean the bathroom.

She lived better alone.

No one could disappoint her then. And she couldn't hurt them when she was on her own.

MONDAY MORNING, Tricia sat at her desk, trying to decide which file to tackle before she left for court. Time to focus on the task at hand, rather than wonder who had torched her mom's shed. She grabbed the top file. The wife had called 911 a couple of times on her husband, but this was the first time she'd agreed to press charges. Tricia scrawled a note to check in with the victim, and make sure she was still hanging in there. It wouldn't hurt to call the anger management counselor and a few other folks. Get their read on the defendant. She rubbed her jawline as she wrote, but she stopped when she reached the ridge of scar tissue on her chin.

Memories of that disastrous relationship seared her mind. Andrew Parker had looked like the right man for her when she bumped into him during a college class. But she should have known better. Now she knew the signs of an abuser. Then she'd been a desperate nineteen-year-old, looking for any man who might offer her a new life far away from her stepfather's house. It hadn't taken long for a pair of baby blue eyes and a great smile to sweep her off her feet as she tried to prove to herself she was lovable after the things her stepfather had done to her. She hadn't known that, over the weeks and months, Andrew's smile would become rare, while his control over her increased.

Her thoughts flitted to the photo she'd looked at the previous week. She grabbed the top folder from Andrew's file and pulled out Linda's picture. She rubbed her scar and reminded herself she'd covered it with concealer. No one saw the larger scar that marred her heart. Or the memories drawn to the surface by Linda Parker's photo. When she looked at it, the bruises made her flash to the ones Andrew had beaten into her.

Tricia pushed her chair away from the desk, stomach spinning, and leaned her head back. She used to love her job. Now she vacillated between satisfaction and a weighted-down feeling. The burden amplified with each new case tossed on her desk.

Sydney stepped into her office. "You're looking at that file again."

"Which one?" Tricia casually covered the file name.

"The Parker file. The one that depresses you each time you examine it. What happened to the attorney who was passionate about her job, protecting victims and bringing justice to abusers?"

Tricia sighed. That was the question she wrestled with each day. The Parker case had pushed her to the breaking point. "She's still buried in here somewhere."

"You need to find a way to love your job again." Sydney leaned on the desk, looking Tricia in the eye. "No job is worth the misery on your face. I need my friend back."

Sydney was right. "I'll pray about it."

"Do." Sydney smiled then turned to leave. "I've got to get to a motion in an hour. See you there."

Tricia nodded.

Somehow she had to take joy in the small victories rather than focusing on the fact that domestic violence hadn't ended and likely never would. She could help victims—one at a time—reclaim control of their lives. Ignore yet again the reality that she'd lived the life herself.

A knock pulled her from her thoughts, and Tricia opened her eyes to find a paralegal pointing at her watch.

"You'll be late for court if you don't leave."

Tricia glanced at her watch and bolted to her feet. "Are the files ready?"

"On the corner of my desk, sorted by attorney."

"Thanks."

Time to put her doubts behind her and head to court. Flip the switch. Transform herself into a mentally tough and prepared opponent. Someone other attorneys had to reckon with.

Tricia stood and grabbed the pile off the paralegal's desk. A tumbleweed of tension roiled in her stomach. She exhaled and prayed the sensation would pass. Her thoughts wandered as she approached the courthouse and finally the courtroom. Attorneys and clients talked in hushed tones in clusters scattered around the hallway. Tension vibrated in the air. She steeled herself against it and prayed for wisdom and favor before pushing open the solid oak, carved door.

Controlled chaos reigned in the courtroom. She relaxed, as something about the atmosphere turned her discomfort into charged anticipation. She loved trial work for that very reason. One never knew what would happen, even in hearings as seemingly insignificant as scheduling a trial date.

Her gaze swept the room. The high ceilings were inlaid with round rosettes. The jury box, witness stand, attorney tables and judge's bench were all stained mahogany. Judge Sinclair's attention focused on the dueling attorneys in front of her. With her chestnut hair pulled behind her ears and glasses perched on her nose, she had the air of a middle-aged librarian. Tricia had learned not to underestimate the judge's brains or her dedication to helping women and children.

Tricia brushed past the bar separating the gallery from the action and edged through the crush of bodies to find a corner of the plaintiff's table to stack her files. After releasing the files, she flexed her fingers and eyed the line.

Easily a dozen attorneys stood in front of her, some with clients. All waiting for their chance to stand in front of the judge. Tricia grabbed her first folder from the pile and quickly reviewed the file. The front sheet contained important dates and status information. Time to schedule this one for a hearing if defense counsel appeared as ordered. A quick scan of the room didn't reveal opposing counsel, so Tricia picked up the next file.

The defendant in this case had decided his two-year-old made a good punching bag. She swallowed hard against the rush of anger. Somehow she must remain professional and detached, though everything in her wanted to ask the man how he could do such things to a defenseless child. She skimmed the file and stilled when she saw Noah Brust's name listed as a witness. She glanced up and scanned the room. Was he here? There. His lanky, yet muscular, form leaned against the wall. He was frowning, arms crossed across his defined chest, tightness around his eyes as he scanned the room. She knew how he felt. These kind of cases made you question the human race. The world should be safe for children, but too often wasn't.

He looked up and caught her eye. The blood fled her face at the realization he'd spotted her. Then he nodded, and something electric sizzled between them as the rest of the room faded into the distance. Her mind should be on the case, not him, yet heat flooded her face under his appraisal.

Tricia forced her gaze back to the file. She thought she'd moved past her attraction when he'd pushed her firmly away after the trial. After meeting him, she'd allowed herself to believe he might be the one. They'd gotten along so well from the moment they'd met. She'd wanted to trust him and let go of her past. Hope for a relationship filled with happiness.

She sneaked another peek at him. He was still watching her, but the frown didn't exude anger. Instead, he seemed thoughtful. What did that mean? She shook her head. Her energy should be focused on this case right now even if it took a monumental effort. Tricia rolled her shoulders and then looked at the file. She scanned the photos, and tears flooded her eyes as she took in the nurse's photographs of the child. She swallowed hard to stop the tears that threatened as the bruises and odd angle of his arm suggested it was broken. Opposing counsel would not see how much the images of the tyke affected her:

A musky cologne flowed over her, tickling her throat and nearly making her choke. The stench could only mean Earl Montgomery stood next to her. The thought of fighting the odor during the Parker trial turned her stomach. She closed the file and took a step back as she turned. "Good morning, Earl."

Maybe he'd leave and take the strong aroma with him if she could get him to talk quickly.

"It's been a while, little lady."

She crossed her arms. "All of a week. What do you need?"

"I'd like to discuss the Parker matter. Rumor has it you're the attorney." He fidgeted with the lapels of his gaudy plaid jacket.

Tricia stared at him. "Have been since the beginning."

"Trial's around the corner."

She waited. What did he expect her to say?

"It's never too late to be reasonable. You know the guy didn't do it. If anything, your client started the argument. In fact, I have it on good authority that she's not willing to testify anymore." He brushed a few strands of stringy hair over the top of his bald head. He rocked back on his heels and grinned at her as if he expected her to roll over at his words.

"And how would you know? Interfering with my witness?"

"Just doing my trial prep, little lady."

Tricia ground her teeth at the familiarity and the condescending tone. "He broke her jaw. Usually the woman wants to see her abuser in jail."

"Maybe. But I've always known you to be reasonable when presented with the truth." His oily smile made her want to back away.

She stiffened. Earl wouldn't understand why she would not give up on Linda. She had to keep Andrew from hurting anyone else.

Drawing a deep breath, Tricia met his gaze. "Thanks for the suggestion, Earl. Much as you might like me to accept that this is Linda's final decision, I'll talk to her first."

"No problem, darling." He waved toward the gallery. "There she is."

Tricia turned to follow where he pointed. Her gaze stopped when it landed on Noah. His eyes seemed to warm as they locked with hers. It had been nearly a year since he'd looked at her like that, and it flustered her. She felt heat climb her cheeks and had to force herself to blink and move past him. The moment she did she felt as if the day had grown colder.

To his right, Linda stood stiffly against the back wall chewing on a fingernail. One look at her face and sloped shoulders was enough. She really wanted to drop the charges. Tricia smiled at the woman. She could handle this. It had happened before and would happen again. All the more reason to make sure she spent time with Linda, made sure she felt prepared for next week.

"State's not dropping the charges, Earl. Hope you're ready for trial next week."

Linda avoided eye contact as Tricia approached. Her perfectly coiffed hair and tailored pantsuit didn't match the nervous gesture of her nail biting or the extra lines etched around her eyes.

"Linda?" The woman looked up, gaze scanning the area around them as if waiting for Andrew to appear out of the woodwork. "What is it? What's wrong?"

"I don't know if I can do this." Linda's manicured hands twisted. "He's threatening terrible things if I go through with this."

Tricia took a deep breath, prayed for the right words. "I know you're scared."

"No. You have no idea what this is like. Lying in bed each night wondering if he'll violate the protective order. If he'll break into his own house, and beat me again for going to the police." Tricia knew exactly what it was like to live with that kind of fear...but she couldn't say that.

Linda would never respect her if she knew it was Tricia's fault that Andrew had been free to hurt her. No, she'd have to go with her usual, logical arguments. "If you don't stand up to him now, he will abuse you again."

Linda's face collapsed. "But he's promised to do better."

"Has he promised that before?" She knew too well the verbal punches that preceded the physical, followed by empty promises.

The quiet question hung in the air. Tricia let it settle, willing Linda to think of every other promise, every plea for forgiveness. A tear streaked a course down Linda's cheek. Tricia pulled a tissue from her pocket and handed it to Linda.

"What will we do?"

"You and your boys will build a new life. One without fear."

"It's not that easy."

"I know, but you have to start somewhere. Testify next Monday and make that the next step in finding freedom from Andrew."

Linda shook her head, the blond waves shielding her face. "I can't."

"Yes, you can." Tricia took a deep breath. "Linda, I know you can do this." Tricia paused. Should she say more? No, not now. No need to add to Linda's concerns. "Together we can show the judge and jury what Andrew is really like. Encourage them to put him behind bars. But I can't do that without your testimony."

Linda wiped the tissue under each eye and took a shuddering breath. Squaring her shoulders, she nodded. "I'll do it."

Tricia struggled not to visibly sag in relief and instead project the image of the accomplished attorney who'd expected nothing less.

Linda smiled weakly and walked away, crossing paths as she exited with Sam Tucker, the opposing attorney on the child abuse case, arriving late as usual. Tricia turned to head to the front of the courtroom as well, but before she could walk away, her eyes met Noah's. The open appreciation and admiration in his gaze flustered her just as much now as it had a year earlier. Taking a deep breath, she forced herself to focus. Aside from the arson investigation, Noah Brust was nothing to her but someone from her past. She wouldn't let him be anything else.

If she could take Andrew on in court, surely she could take on her heart.

5

M*onday*

Noah raced his pickup to the fire station, images of Tricia muddying his thoughts. She'd looked so beautiful as she'd talked to the other woman, comforting and encouraging her yet with a firmness that one could lean into and trust.

He kept thinking about her conversation. The woman had trembled, as if afraid of something. Or someone. Tricia had used a low voice and a soothing tone to talk the woman out of her fear. In fact, she'd straightened and agreed to everything Tricia said. The fear had disappeared when the woman walked out of the courtroom. Then he'd noticed Tricia's tremors. What she'd said and done had drained her.

He'd had the strangest urge to reach out to her, comfort her. The woman poured herself into each case. Even when it stripped her to the core. Maybe he'd judged her too harshly. How could he doubt her dedication to her cases after what he'd witnessed?

The thing that got him was the aura of sadness around her when she looked at him. As if she felt the same pull he did, but understood the chasm between them. One he had dug spoonful by bitter spoonful. Discomfort filled him, a sensation he hated. He whipped the truck into an open parking slot and hopped out as wolf whistles assaulted him.

"Overslept, Brust?" Graham Jackson slouched in a chair, his tall frame plopped in front of an open bay door.

"I wish. I got to waste another morning in court waiting to be called for a hearing they postponed right before the judge swore me in." Noah rolled his neck. The muscles had knotted tight while he waited. Courtrooms would never number among his favorite places to spend time, but were often a necessary part of it. "Don't do anything crazy while I check in." Noah sauntered into the office, then sagged against the door. He hated court. Hated the inefficiency of the system. Dated the taste it left in his mouth. Hated the bitter memories.

The bell rang loud enough to stop a bull in its tracks. He grinned as adrenaline started its surge through him. He opened the door and raced to his cubby.

"What are we looking at?"

Graham shrugged into his turnout coat. "Dispatch says a fire at a residence. Sounds like a detached building."

Good. They could contain the fire before it spread, minimizing the damage. Noah pulled on his boots and coat before slapping his helmet on his head.

"Brust." A gravelly voice yelled his name.

Noah stopped mid-slap and looked up. Weary stood in the back of the bay, staring at him. Surely Weary wasn't about to stop him from leaving with his men. "Yes?"

"Come with me."

Graham looked at Noah. One truck barreled out of the bay, lights flashing. "We can't wait."

Noah nodded.

"Are you serious about learning fire investigation?" Challenge filled Weary's voice as if he expected Noah to fail before he really started.

He stiffened his back as the wail of the first truck faded in the distance.

"We can't wait any longer. Either hop on or go with him."

Noah groaned. He lived for fighting fires, working toward the goal of surpassing his father's reputation, an impossible task from the sidelines. His knee throbbed, making his decision for him. Better to investigate than let someone decide he needed a medical leave. Again.

"Go ahead." Noah slapped the side of the truck.

The last man leapt on the truck, and Noah watched it race from the garage, sirens blaring.

"This better be good." He mumbled under his breath.

"What, Brust?"

Noah found Weary standing in front of him. "How do you do that?"

"Life's all about making probies jump. Come on." The man turned and walked away.

"I am not a probie."

Weary snorted. "You are in my program."

Noah clamped his hands on his hips and fought the urge to hit something. He tried to get the adrenaline to subside as he stripped off his protective gear and placed his helmet back on its hook. He'd thought the day couldn't get any worse. Who knew what Mr. Sunshine had in mind for his afternoon?

When Noah entered Weary's office, the man sat behind his desk. He'd propped his feet on the desk, and was flipping through a stack of photos.

"What are those?"

"Wrong question to ask."

Silence filled the room except for the sound of Weary shuffling the top photo to the bottom of the pile, replacing it with the next again and again. Noah clamped his jaw against the urge to spout words.

Finally, he couldn't take the silence anymore. "And the right question..."

"Where are these pictures from? What do they show?" Weary

pulled his legs off the desk and lurched forward in his chair. He tossed a couple at Noah. "What do you see?"

Noah juggled the images. Why look at photos when he'd spent hours at the site? He tried to focus on them, but didn't know what he was looking at. He bit his tongue. The shot looked like a close-up of a shed's concrete floor. Swirls of iridescent colors ran through a liquid pooled on one part of the concrete. Gasoline or oil mixed with water?

Weary cleared his throat. "Guesses?"

"Something leaked gas or oil there."

"The cause?"

"Lawn mower stored there? Other small, gas-run tool?"

"Do you think this fire started on its own?"

Noah shrugged. "Probably not. But..."

"But we investigate first. Rule out other causes of the fire. Never walk in assuming arson. You have to keep an open mind or you'll miss key details and evidence because they don't fit your model."

Noah paused and studied the picture more. "I still say this looks like evidence of gas or another accelerant used to start the fire. But..."

"But it could be caused by any number of things." Brian Weary leaned back in his chair, a grimace on his face. "Welcome to fire investigation. The liquid could be from a lawn mower. Or it could be remnants of what an arsonist used to start the fire. There's the challenge. Determining the cause." He swiveled in his chair, pointed at a map taped to the wall behind his desk. "See that? Each pin represents a fire we've investigated this year. Orange represents arson. Green electrical. Blue lightning. You get the idea. See anything unusual?"

Noah stepped closer to the desk and leaned against it to get a closer look. "You've got quite a few arsons. More than usual."

"Yep." Weary leaned back, locking his hands behind his head. "It's too early to tell much, but those grass fires on the outskirts of town could be connected to your shed fire. *If* it's arson."

Noah rubbed his jaw and tried to memorize the map. He had so much to learn.

Weary grabbed a thick binder from the floor behind his desk. He tossed the volume at Noah, who lunged to catch it before paper flew from it. "Remember the photo. I want you to figure out what it is. This book should help."

Noah looked from the photos to the book. "You want me to use this?"

Weary put his glasses on the tip of his nose and looked over them at Noah. Then he pivoted his chair until Noah stared at his back.

Heat filled Noah's face. "Fine," he muttered. He stood and stalked from the room with the photos and binder.

Everybody had warned him that Weary was unpredictable and bordered on mean. Why had he thought his experience with the man would be different? Noah plopped down at one of the tables in the kitchen area, binder falling to the table. He opened the volume and started flipping through the pages. He needed to calm down or the words would swim as he read. After trying to focus on the formulas and photos for an hour, he stood and paced the room. He needed some fresh oxygen pumping to his brain before he pitched the book in the trash, but somehow Weary would know he'd stepped away and might not see it as a helpful brain break.

He strode to the refrigerator and grabbed a bottle of water then returned to the table where he slumped. The rumble of a truck pulling into a bay across the large garage grabbed his attention.

"Weary get to you already?" Graham pulled out and then straddled a chair, his face covered in soot and his body reeking of a fire. He feigned a look of concern, but his eyes danced with laughter.

"Don't say it."

"I told you so?" Graham shook his head. "I wouldn't think of it."

Noah rubbed his hands over his head. "Can you believe he wants me to study this?" He wanted to kick the thick volume back to Weary's office. He'd signed up to read fires, not tomes.

"It's just a book."

Yeah. For anyone else. But how could Noah hide his dyslexia? Studying in a group was one thing. But he doubted he'd find an audio version for this volume.

Graham flipped it open. "Look, there are even pictures."

"I guess that's all I need. Find a picture that matches this one." Noah tossed the photo to Graham. "Out of eight hundred pages."

"No problem." He flipped a couple of pages, then pushed it back to Noah. "I'm sure you'll find the match in a few days."

Noah snorted. "Thanks for the encouragement."

"That's what I'm here for." Graham slapped the table and stood. "Let me know if you need help."

Noah rubbed his knee where it throbbed. He couldn't afford to let this opportunity go. If he couldn't fight fires the rest of his life, then he'd settle for determining cause.

Noah pushed back from the table, and paced the room. He locked his hands behind his head and concentrated on breathing. A steady in and out pattern. He knew the pattern in the water. Weary had asked an impossible question. Noah couldn't determine whether the gas existed at the site prior to the fire.

Yep, this was a test. Weary was seeing where he'd run with this. Noah could waltz back into Weary's office with a tale of woe and find himself forever cut out of investigative work. Definitely not what he wanted.

A woman walked past the window. Her head tilted away from him so he couldn't see her features. But her dark-brown hair reminded him of Tricia Jamison. Once the thought took hold, he couldn't shake it. He didn't want to think of her. Couldn't think of her. Needed to think about the picture. But all he saw in his mind's eye was Tricia.

A woman he had misjudged and unjustly pushed away. A woman he needed to forgive.

And a woman he needed to ask to forgive him.

6

W*ednesday*

Judge Sinclair looked down her glasses at Tricia, then turned her attention to Earl Montgomery. "You're here for the pretrial on this case, correct?"

"Yes, your honor." Earl caressed his Kelly-green paisley tie. "My client, Andrew Parker, requests a continuance in this matter."

"Reasons?"

"We have been unable to locate a witness."

"Who is this witness?"

A shadow flashed across Earl's face. "A buddy from college my client spent time with the night of the alleged incident."

Tricia tried not to smile too broadly. She knew the real reason—Linda had agreed to testify, and Andrew wanted more time to wear her back down. No way would she let that happen. "Your honor, this case has been pending before this court for months, more than enough time for Mr. Montgomery and his client to locate this witness. In fact, I don't believe they have any witnesses listed on their evidentiary motion, so the witness would be excluded for that reason." Tricia glanced at the summary sheet, and confirmed her memory. "This is no valid reason to delay the trial."

"Other than Mr. Parker receiving a fair trial. His wife may be unwilling to press the charges."

"Counsel?" The judge looked at Tricia.

"I talked with her yesterday and verified that she will testify. Even without her testimony, the state is ready to proceed."

"Is Mrs. Parker here?"

"No. This is supposed to be a routine pretrial hearing."

Judge Sinclair looked over her glasses at Tricia. "Then we'll see her at trial. Defendant's motion is denied. Thank you, counsel."

Earl collected his files and turned toward the doors. "See you next week, little lady."

Tricia fought the urge to go wash her hands. He made her feel so slimy.

The cell phone sang the theme to Monday Night Football from some deep recess of her purse. Caleb's ringtone. She grabbed the bag and scrabbled through it for the phone as she walked back to her office.

"Hey..." Huffing cut off her words.

"Can you come to my house?" Caleb's words rushed on top of each other.

Sirens blared in the background, causing her to push the phone closer to her ear. "What?"

"How fast can you get to my house?"

"Half an hour."

"See you then." He hung up, and Tricia stared at the silent phone. She entered the elevator of County City building and pushed the button for her floor.

Before she could toss the phone back in the recesses of her bag, it rang again, this time the standard tone. She glanced at the display and stilled when she saw the caller was Dani Richards. Why would her brother's girlfriend call? Especially on the heels of her brother?

She opened the phone. "Dani?"

"Has Caleb reached you?"

"Just did. What's going on?"

"There's trouble at his place." Dani's voice sounded muffled, as if she were rushing somewhere. A car door slammed.

"Are you sure?" Tricia exited the elevator and headed down the hallway to her small office.

"Does your brother joke about things like this?"

"No."

"Then we'll meet you there."

Tricia paused at her office door. "All right."

Snatching her briefcase from next to her desk, she shoved the Parker file inside it, then headed back down the hall and out of the office. She prayed that Caleb was okay as she reached her car and headed out of town down O Street.

Blood thundered in her ears as her heart raced. What-if scenarios ran through her mind. What if he'd injured himself? What if one of the men he'd investigated had come after him? What if...

~

NOAH OPENED the door to his second-floor apartment, the autumn wind raking across him from the open patio door. He shivered as it penetrated his sweat-soaked shirt. Bicycling around Holmes Lake left him worn out, but in a good way. His body had cooperated with his mind and allowed him to exercise the way he'd wanted. His knee had even kept up.

He wiped his forearm across his forehead, swiping sweat. The exercise had succeeded in drawing off remnants of adrenaline from another shift. Now he could anticipate forty-eight hours off duty.

He walked into the kitchen and was pouring a glass of water when the scanner screeched to life. A voice crackled into the room. "Fire units, forty-one reported...." static interrupted. Noah frowned and wrote down the address after the static cleared. Weary wanted him on call to investigate fire scenes until Weary or another investigator arrived. Guess this fire would qualify.

The address he'd jotted down was outside Lincoln. Why would Lincoln units respond? Maybe the volunteer fire department had responded to another fire, leaving it unavailable. Or the fire was blazing out of control. He fidgeted as his mind raced.

His phone vibrated. He pulled up the text message. *Report to fire—Caleb Jamison's home. Weary.*

A sinking sensation filled his gut. A fire at Officer Caleb Jamison's house? That wouldn't be good, though it would explain Lincoln Fire Department's participation. Noah sucked air through his teeth in a whistle. Jamison's mother's fire had been small. Now this? He needed to get to the scene stat. No waiting for the flames to die down. The radio continued to blare as he raced to his bathroom. Ten minutes later he walked out of his apartment, hair still wet but with the address in hand.

The miles flew by as he sped out of town to the scene.

For the last stretch, he followed a blue Miata down the winding roads. Noah flew around the curves as he stayed behind the Miata on the path to the fire. What firefighter in his right mind drove a car like that? He much preferred his truck for a sense of safety.

The sports car slowed as it neared the turnoff, then stopped in front of flashing lights. Noah blocked the car in, and hurried out of his vehicle. A woman stepped from the Miata. Her dark hair swirled around her face in the wind. She turned toward him as she tried to shake the hair from her face. Time slowed when he identified the driver he'd followed. Tricia Jamison froze in place as he stared at her.

"Stay back here." He started to walk past her, then turned. "It might not be safe up there."

"I have to get to Caleb." She shivered, and then wrapped her arms around her small frame. "He called." The words trailed off.

Again, Noah fought the urge to take her into his arms, provide some reassurance. The instinct surprised him. No woman had ever distracted him from a fire before. Instead of reaching for her the way he wanted to, he spun around and left her standing there, feeling like a heel as he walked away, hating himself every second.

He had a job to do. Before she became the next target, he needed to figure out who was starting these fires and why.

Comforting her would have to wait, no matter how much he

wanted to support her. He had to do his job first. He had to gather the evidence. Piece it together. Figure out who had started the fires that targeted Tricia's mother...and her brother...and might target her next.

The fire had fully engulfed the garage. An explosion split the air as windows shattered outward.

7

W*ednesday*

Tricia felt the cold seeping through her clothes and into her bones.

Firemen hustled toward Caleb's garage, hoses hoisted over their shoulders. One already had water trained on the flames.

The strobing lights of the fire trucks pounded into her head as they pulsed. She tried to turn away, but felt the magnetic pull. She shook her head, trying to clear the distractions. She had to find Caleb.

Where was he?

"Tricia, you made it."

Tricia turned at the voice of Dani Richards, the best thing that had happened to her big brother.

"Have you seen Caleb?" Tricia couldn't move any closer to the action.

"No. I just got arrived." Dani searched the scene as she grabbed Tricia. "Come on. We can't wait here."

Tricia knew Dani was right, but that didn't make it easier to move. *Please, God.* Her mind couldn't form more words. Her gaze found Noah again as he wove past the first fire truck and walked toward the partially obscured log cabin, Caleb's pride and joy. Caleb joined Noah, and she felt light-headed. He was okay. The men shook hands, then Noah gestured toward her.

Time to get up there.

Tricia swallowed. "Guess they want us."

Dani nodded, and Tricia forced her way forward. At Mom's she'd smelled the smoke. This time she could see the flames as well as breathe the acrid scent. Her shoulders relaxed. The fire hadn't reached the house yet. The firefighters had reached the home in time to confine it to the detached garage.

She shivered as she reached Caleb. "Is this an escalation?"

Caleb put an arm around Dani, then stared at Tricia. "What makes you say that?"

"At Mom's house it was a shed in the backyard. The fire couldn't do much damage. This..." She pointed at the garage. "A few more minutes and the house could have caught fire." She rubbed her hands on her arms, trying to generate some warmth inside.

"I don't know, Trish." He watched the fire with her. "The fires may not be connected."

Tricia snorted. "You don't really believe that."

"I want to, but you're right. I can't. These fires were deliberate. Someone is targeting our family."

A large man huffed over to their sides. Todd Westmont? Wasn't that his name? One of Caleb's fellow officers.

"Jamison, I think you'll want to see this." Westmont gestured away from the garage to the cabin.

Caleb followed the man to the side of the house. Tricia started to follow them until Noah walked up to their party. He'd actually sounded concerned about her earlier, but maybe that was a fluke. She fought the temptation to avoid him, even if that would leave things on a friendlier note. What did he want anyway?

TRICIA STARTED TOWARD THE GROUP, back stiff. Noah couldn't tell why, but she'd seemed fine until he'd joined the group.

She seemed to collect herself as she approached. She threw a sweet smile at the officer standing next to Caleb. "Officer Westmont?" She extended her hand to him. "What did you find?"

Westmont pinked at the top of his ears. He rubbed a hand across the back of his neck. "Not sure I can tell you, ma'am." He looked from Tricia to Caleb, who stood with his arms crossed as humor flashed in his eyes.

"Go ahead and let her know. She'll find out soon enough."

"See this over here?" Westmont pointed at some heavy imprints in the soil below a window. "Unless you did something out here recently, Caleb, looks like someone thought about going into your house and then changed his mind."

"Maybe he noticed the security system." Noah pointed at a security box visible through the window.

"Maybe." Caleb didn't sound convinced.

The three guys squatted to inspect the imprints while Tricia and Dani watched.

"I think he decided to go for the easier target."

Noah looked up at Tricia's soft words. "Why?"

"Look. There's a window, but it's high and fairly small. It doesn't take much to realize that Caleb has a security system in place. But how many people have one in the garage? It was also clear Caleb wasn't here, so if you want to damage someone's property a garage works." Noah stared at her, and she shrugged. "I thought about it during the drive."

Maybe she had a point.

Officer Westmont pointed at the ground. "There's not much we can cast for footprints, but I'll have the crime scene folks come take photos and see what they can do."

Noah straightened. What was the protocol? Who owned the scene—the fire department or the police? Caleb seemed to read his mind.

"I think we can work together on this one, don't you, Brust?" Caleb's face left no question about the correct answer.

Tricia stood silhouetted against the sun. Multicolored leaves fell around her from the maple trees in the backyard. As he looked at her, he had the uncomfortable sense that whatever was going on, it wasn't over yet. And he didn't like the direction his thoughts took him.

~

ANOTHER FIRE. The smell stung her nose, and it wasn't the pleasant smell of fall leaves burning. Tricia shuddered to think what would have happened if Caleb hadn't had an alarm system. The thought of his home rather than his garage burning...the outcome could have been so much worse.

After watching the men for a while, Tricia found a quiet corner of the block and called the office. She had the Parker file with her and promised to get some work done, but she couldn't face going back to the office. Not drained like this.

She didn't know what to brace for next. First, the fire at her mother's house. Now this one. Both events felt like specific attacks against those she loved. Add the Parker trial into the mix and the nightmares it resurrected, and she felt defenseless.

When the firefighters had the fire under control and she knew it wouldn't spread to the house, she left Caleb's. He didn't need any help. And he didn't need her comfort when Dani was there, even if it meant Logan Collins, the photojournalist Dani worked with in her job as a TV news reporter, shot video in the background. Looked like Caleb's fire would make the Channel 13 evening newscasts.

Amid all the activity, Tricia felt hollow. Like she had nothing of worth to offer.

So she left.

She'd learned that much from her past. When the situation got tough, the best she could hope for was distance. Protect herself from the pain she'd feel if she stayed.

While the impressions under the window left her worried,

she didn't know how to communicate the churning in her stomach to Caleb. He'd try to play the big brother and get overprotective, maybe even assign someone to watch her house in case she was the next target. But hovering wasn't what she needed. She wanted someone to hear her. Understand her fears —understand *her.*

She pulled into the driveway and parked the car. Her small cottage called to her—today it felt like a place of solitude and refuge from the terrible things people did to each other. No one could hurt her here. And she could avoid others' pain for a time. She grabbed her mail from the metal box next to the door, unlocked the door and entered her sanctuary. She flipped through the pile before tossing it on the dining room table.

Her white-and-blue chintz couch beckoned her from the living room. She kicked off her navy heels and entered the sunny room. She lay down on the couch, letting the cushions form around her body, and closed her eyes.

The peaceful room had no effect on her mind. It still raced with questions, theories, suppositions. With a groan she got up, fiddled with the photos lining her entertainment center and then checked the plants for water.

Someone had targeted her family.

The perpetrator thought he had a good reason. Surely he understood the danger in targeting the family and home of a LPD investigator. The cost ran too high to do it without a strong motivation. She needed to find him before something else... something worse...happened. She sank against the couch cushions and stared at the blank top sheet of the legal pad. Her thoughts cycled like birds caught in the wind. Nothing stuck as she doodled on the page. A chill shook her, and she tugged an afghan from the back of the couch down over her. She'd close her eyes for one moment. Just long enough to regain focus.

A vibration pulled her from a restless dream. She slipped her phone from her pocket. "Hello?"

"Hey, Tricia." Dani Richard's peppy broadcasting voice filtered from the cell. "I'm headed to your house. Be ready for me to pick you up in ten minutes."

"What?"

"I decided it's time for some therapy, and you're joining me."

"What about your job?"

"Logan will finish the packages for me. You know he's better at it than I am." Dani sighed. "Besides I can't stop thinking about the fire at Caleb's. What if he'd been home? I need a distraction. How about coffee and some shopping?"

Tricia felt a smile bubble up. "I was in the middle of therapy."

"Napping doesn't count. Besides you've held out on me."

"No, I haven't."

"A set of blue eyes glued to you tells me differently. See you in a minute."

Tricia couldn't decide whether to groan or grin. She wasn't ready to discuss Noah with anyone, especially not an expert interviewer like Dani. But stopping Dani once she had an idea in her head took the energy of stopping a college linebacker. Might as well give in gracefully. By the time Dani pulled up, Tricia waited on her front step. She stood and hurried to the car.

"Where are we headed?"

"Southpointe. We'll get a little fresh air while we shop."

Tricia thought about the outfit sitting in her closet, unworn; the fruit of their last shopping therapy session. "All right."

Traffic flowed well as Dani zipped toward the outdoor mall. Tricia tried to focus on Dani's chatter, but found herself pulled between thoughts of the Parker trial and the fires. Dani didn't care that Tricia's mind was elsewhere; she chattered away in a clear effort to distract her from her thoughts.

Dani pulled her in and out of shops until Tricia's feet throbbed.

"I thought you said coffee was the focus of this adventure." Tricia groaned. "Dani, I can't smell another candle or try on another blouse. Not today."

Dani put her hands on her hips and frowned. Her face quivered, and Tricia wanted to grab Dani in a hug.

"It'll be okay. Caleb wasn't hurt, Dani."

"I know. But he could have been." Dani straightened her shoulders and swiped under her eyes. "Come on, here's the bookstore."

Tricia grabbed the door and walked in, making a beeline for the coffee shop at the back of the store. She ordered a cafe mocha and then a black coffee for Dani. When she turned around with the cups, Dani had collapsed at a table, the floor around her decorated with shopping bags.

Tricia carried the cups to the table, then sank into the empty chair. "Here you go."

Dani grabbed the cup, took a sip and grimaced. "Black? You must be tired."

"Or I'm punishing you for dragging me all over the mall."

"You won't consider it punishment in a minute."

Tricia waited while Dani got up and doctored her coffee. She tried to relax and enjoy the jazz playing in the store. Usually, she could turn off the world when she was in a bookstore. The pull of other worlds and experiences combined with coffee and good music could transport her far away from her cases and life. Today, all she noticed was the smell of smoke clinging to her clothes. She swirled her mocha around the cup, waiting for it to cool.

She might smell of smoke, but Dani looked wrung out. "Are you okay?"

Dani shook her head. "You'd think I'd understand about Caleb's job. What happened to me last year should have been a wake-up call."

Tricia shuddered at the memory. One of Dani's colleagues had stalked and then kidnapped her with the intention of killing her. Thankfully, Caleb had come to her rescue. "That's a week I hope to never relive." She was glad that the circumstances had brought Dani and Caleb back together years after their initial romance, but the danger of those terrifying days was something she'd rather avoid...if the arsonist currently targeting her family would let her.

Dani dumped two packets of sweetener and a couple of creamers into her cup and stirred it longer than necessary.

"Why don't you spit it out?"

"We've set a date."

Tricia jerked. "You've what?"

"Set a date." Dani extended her left hand. "See? Caleb finally asked me to marry him." A diamond the size of Memorial Stadium winked at Tricia from Dani's finger. He must have eaten a lot of ramen noodles to afford it.

Tricia grabbed Dani's hand and twisted it to view the diamond, an unforced smile on her face for what seemed the first time in weeks. "Oh, my goodness, how did I miss that earlier? He didn't breathe a word."

"I know. Can you believe he actually asked?" Dani's squeal was muted.

Hugs. That's what people did at times like this. What was wrong with her? Tricia leaned over to squeeze Dani. "I'm so happy for you."

"I was so excited...then the fire. Tricia, how often does this happen?"

"Not often."

Dani sipped her coffee and grimaced. "It feels like it's time to redeem the past and all its mistakes, then this. I don't know if I can lose Caleb again."

Tricia's smile faltered. She was thrilled for her best friend. For goodness sake, her brother had finally done it. But past mistakes...Dani and Caleb might have overcome theirs, but Tricia lived with hers.

"Someday you'll find your prince."

Tricia stiffened and schooled her features into a neutral expression, one she'd perfected for court. "What makes you think I want love? Maybe I'm called to the single life."

"Maybe. But a call doesn't mean running scared in the other direction. And I know you want love. God created us with that deep desire to know someone loves us. Treasures us. Yep, you want that, too." Dani propped her chin on her clasped hands, ring blinking. "But you have to risk. Pretty sure that's the first step to a lifelong love."

"It worked so well for you and Caleb." Tricia hated the sarcasm that filled her voice. But how could Dani ignore the baby she'd given up when Caleb left her pregnant and alone years ago when he headed to college? "Don't you ever wish that you'd kept your baby? Or that you'd never been pregnant?"

"Yes." Dani's eyes lost some of their light. "But I'm not talking about the past. I can't change that. I *can* choose whether to live in the past and blame Caleb for my decisions. Or allow forgiveness to cover those decisions and move into the future." Dani swirled her coffee in the cup, watching it play along the sides. Tricia's thoughts felt as muddied as the drink. "Tricia, I've lived in the past. It was ugly. Filled with tears, guilt, denial. Wondering where my daughter is. Hoping, praying she's with a wonderful family." Dani tried to smile. "But I had to leave it behind. If I hadn't, I'd miss today. We'll always regret our early experiences, but we choose to live here now."

Tricia wanted to crawl under the table. "I'm sorry." She looked at the cup in her hands. "I shouldn't have dredged up the past."

Dani grabbed her hand, and Tricia fought tears. "I know something happened. I wish you'd tell me what."

Tricia clenched her jaw. No way would she pour out everything now. Not even to her best friend.

Dani studied her, then nodded. "When you're ready, I'm here. Don't forget that you can turn it over to God." A sheepish smile played on her lips. "Sorry. Who am I to tell you that? You've followed Christ longer than I have."

"That doesn't make me perfect." Tricia was far from there.

8

W*ednesday*

Noah squatted near the smoldering ruins of Jamison's garage. Weary had pulled in after the firefighters killed the flames. Now to determine what happened.

"We'll come back in the morning. The building is too hot to crawl around." Weary nodded toward the far wall. "We'll want to start over there tomorrow."

Noah couldn't figure out why the far wall was special. Weary must have noticed.

"See that flare pattern up the wall? That may signal the initial location of the fire. No guarantees, but as good a spot as any to start." He turned and started walking away. "Brust?"

"Yes, sir?"

"Aren't you coming?"

"Sir?"

"We might not be able to get in the scene yet, but we can definitely start our investigation. Grab your camera. We can get lots of photos before it turns dark. We don't want to miss anything."

Noah sighed. So much for heading home for a few hours on his day off. "Sure."

Caleb followed him to his car. "Any thoughts?"

"None. Did you ask Weary?"

"He's silent as a clam around me." Caleb shoved his hands in his pocket. "This one has me worried. I think Tricia's right."

Noah leaned against his truck. "And?"

"If someone's going after my family, then something triggered this. People don't become arsonists overnight, right?"

"Far as I know."

"And the odds of my mom's house and mine—they're too small to think about. They must be connected."

"Agreed. So what will you do?"

"Other than try to convince my sister to let me station a cop at her house? Go through the newspaper. See if there were any articles connected to my family in the days leading up to Mom's fire. Go through old case files. Try to figure out who might have a reason to be angry at me and out of jail. I'll start with those just released."

"I'm not sure Tricia will go for a guard. Maybe whatever's happened will dry up now." Noah opened the passenger-side door and grabbed his camera.

"I'm not willing to bet her life on it. I have to try to make her see reason."

"Good luck with that. I'll take some photos and let you know if we learn anything. Whoever's doing this needs to leave some evidence for us to chase down. Otherwise, we can determine the cause, but not much else."

"I need you to give it your best, before anything else happens." Caleb rubbed his neck. "I've got a bad feeling. The last time I had one..." A shadow crossed the man's face. "I don't want to experience anything like last year's case again. Especially with Dani. And if I'm the target, she could be the next victim."

"Or Tricia."

Caleb swallowed, his gaze off toward the lake. "Or Tricia."

Noah left Caleb and went back to work. He didn't like the thought that Tricia might be the next target. He'd do what it took to get to the bottom of this case before anything happened to her.

As he took pictures of the charred building and followed Weary counterclockwise around the perimeter of the building, he wondered. She seemed strong, but he'd seen flashes of vulnerability. Moments that revealed a woman scarred by something hidden deep inside. Hints of a frightened woman hiding under the facade of a woman in charge of her destiny.

How would she deal with another attack?

And what would he do if he somehow failed to protect her, just as he'd failed to rescue his father? He pushed the thought away and focused on the photos and paying careful attention to everything Weary did. The man might not talk much, but Noah could still learn.

A restlessness filed Noah the moment he walked in his door a few hours later. He paced up and down the small living room, Jessie's nose at his knee. After he tripped over her again, he grabbed her leash. She sat down, a grin seeming to stretch her face as her tongue hung out.

"You've got it, girl. Time to get out of here." He hooked her to the leash, grabbed a plastic bag and headed out the door. They stepped outside the building and a breeze ruffled Jessie's thick fur. The sunlight had faded, and the streetlights kicked on, casting shadows where the light didn't reach.

Noah turned up his jacket collar and started down the sidewalk. Jessie trotted beside him a minute, then planted her feet and growled. The hackles on her back raised as she stared across the parking lot. Noah followed her line of sight. She normally ignored the people around the apartment building. What had her out of sorts...enough that he sensed it, too?

Jessie strained forward, pulling Noah along. She barked, teeth bared.

His dog did not bark at shadows. Something must be out there to get her this worked up.

"Come on, Jessie." He stepped into the parking lot. Jessie pulled ahead. A shadow moved, and Noah squinted. A man stood next to Noah's truck. "Hey, stop."

The man turned and dropped something that fell with a metallic clatter as he bolted from the truck. The man raced across the parking lot to a vehicle. Noah headed to his truck, intent on finding what the man had dropped. A gas can? Noah glanced over his shoulder and saw the man climbing into a car. He couldn't let the man get away. Not without answering a few questions. Noah tried to chase him, but tripped over Jessie, who lunged toward the vehicle, knocking Noah over and pulling the leash from his hand.

A vehicle raced toward the exit, tires screaming against the asphalt.

"Jessie, come."

She ignored him, running toward the car.

His heart thumped as if the Nebraska Blackshirts had him in their sights, and his mouth went dry as the Sahara. "Jessie, here girl."

The dog didn't even look at him. Instead, she barked.

Time slowed as Jessie darted toward the car. It clipped her, throwing the dog into the air. She yelped. Noah stared, not wanting to believe his eyes.

Jessie lay limp on the asphalt.

The driver silhouetted by a streetlight.

Car engine of a dark-colored sedan revving.

Tires spinning.

Then the car flew into reverse and disappeared around the corner.

"Jessie!" Noah scrambled across the pavement toward the dog, ignoring the rocks that cut through his jeans and scraped his hands.

Noah pulled Jessie toward him.

"Hey, mister. Need help?" A teenage boy in a hooded sweatshirt bounded toward him.

"Call 911." Noah's mind jumped in a dozen different directions. The car had hit Jessie. The man had a gas can. Could it be related to the arsons? But why come here? Noah racked his mind trying to think, but his mind had blanked. He needed to get someone else here to look at this until his thoughts cleared. Noah drew his cell phone out of a pocket and pulled up the number he'd programmed in a few days ago.

"Hello?" Background noise almost drowned out Tricia's voice.

"Tricia? This is Noah. Why are you answering your brother's phone?" His words picked up speed. Jessie looked so still. Police lights split the darkness, and he stared at the phone. Everything seemed so harsh and chaotic. The only thing that sounded calm was Tricia's voice in his ear.

~

TRICIA PUSHED a finger against her ear, trying to hear Noah against the backdrop of so much noise at Grisanti's. He needed Caleb? That didn't make sense. "Caleb has pizza all over his hands. Where are you?"

"At my apartment."

"What's going on?" Caleb studied her, his arm draped across Dani's shoulders.

Tricia covered the mouth of her phone. "Noah Brust."

"Give me the phone." Caleb snatched it from her hand before she could do anything.

Dani rolled her eyes and mouthed *sorry*.

Tricia shrugged. It wasn't the first time Caleb had played the overbearing big brother. "So much for our celebration dinner."

"Based on what Caleb and I do, I'm shocked we got this much time to celebrate our engagement." Dani played with her necklace. "Is everything okay?"

"You'll have to ask Caleb. He took the phone before I could ask for more information." Noah had sounded shaken. Tricia itched to hear if he needed help. But first, she needed to pay. Tricia flagged down their waitress and asked for the check. Might as well get ready to leave.

"All right. I'll be there in five minutes." Caleb closed the phone and put it away. "Noah saw someone near his truck. The person dropped a gas can before bolting out of there, hitting his dog on the way out of the parking lot. Sounds like something I should check out."

"Hit his dog?" Her heart ached for Noah at the thought.

"Yes. I need to get over there. Thanks for dinner, Sis. We'll have to do it again soon." Caleb leaned over and brushed a kiss against Dani's forehead.

Dani's brow wrinkled. "Why call you?"

"Noah wants me to check it out in case it's somehow connected to the fires at Mom's house and my cabin."

She reached for her phone. "I'll call this in."

Tricia stood, along with Caleb. "I think I'll follow you." Dani quirked an eyebrow, and Tricia blushed. "I want to make sure his dog is okay."

"Sure." Dani turned away from the table to talk into her phone.

"Come on, Trish. We need to get rolling."

Tricia hurried to keep up with Caleb as he wound his way through the Italian restaurant. She couldn't explain why she needed to see Noah. Why she needed to know he was okay.

All she knew was she wouldn't rest until she was certain.

9

Wednesday

Tricia hopped in her Miata and followed Caleb as he raced east on O Street the couple blocks to 70th. Before long she pulled into Noah's apartment complex near Holmes Lake. Once there, she followed the flashing lights.

She parked the car in a slot, and hopped out. Where were Noah and Jessie? She looked around, trying to find them in the rush of activity.

Caleb had pulled in ahead of her and joined an officer taking a statement from a hooded boy, his arms gesturing in the air. Clusters of people hung back a few feet from the sidewalk, taking in the action. This wasn't a part of Lincoln that typically had incidents requiring the police.

Past the crowd, another officer crouched on the ground next to a man holding a dog. The only movement came when the dog licked the man's hand, then laid her head back down on his lap.

Tricia grabbed her phone, locked the car and hurried toward them. When her heels clicked against the sidewalk, Noah looked up and blinked.

"You're here." His mouth opened and shut as though he didn't know what to say.

"Yes. Caleb told me what happened. I thought you might need help."

"Thank you." He stroked Jessie's fur, then stumbled to his feet. "Can you take Jessie to the emergency vet? The police have more questions before I can leave. She's in pain." Jessie whined as if to reinforce his point.

Tricia looked at the lanky dog, then at her car. "Do you think she'll fit?"

Noah shook his head. "No way she'll fit unless you let her drive."

Tricia puffed her cheeks and bit her tongue. "Other thoughts?" Jessie's whimper broke Tricia's heart. "Give me your keys, and let's put her in your vehicle. She'll fit in it, right?"

Noah nodded and struggled to his feet, cooing at the dog the whole time. He stopped when he reached a large truck. "Here. It's an automatic—keys are in the ignition. The vet is over by Bryan Memorial Hospital. Here's my credit card."

Tricia hopped in while he laid the dog on the passenger's seat. "Give me your cell number, and I'll call you as soon as I know something."

He rattled off the number, and she eased out of the parking space. The dog lay on the seat, barely moving. When she slammed on the brakes, the dog looked at her with sad eyes. "Sorry, girl. I'll drive more carefully."

She drove the streets around the hospital until she finally located the vet, whose office was tucked behind the road. A tech grabbed the dog, while she filled in paperwork. How did they expect her to answer all the questions about a dog she'd just met? She sighed and guessed.

Her phone vibrated in her pocket, and she grabbed it. "Hello?"

"Any word?" A frantic tone laced Noah's words.

"Not yet, but that's good news, right?"

"It shouldn't take long if nothing's wrong with her."

"They're being thorough. Making sure everything's checked out before they send her home. Liability and all."

"Yeah, lawyers run amok."

Tricia sucked in a breath, and silence dangled between them. "Look..."

"I'm sorry." Noah's cleared his throat. "I need to know she's okay."

"Do you want to come get her?"

"Can't. You've got my truck."

"And you've got my car."

Noah cleared his throat again.

"What?" A really bad feeling filled Tricia.

"That's something we need to talk about."

"Why?"

"You parked in a resident's spot, and he called a tow truck."

"Why didn't you stop him?" This was not what she wanted to deal with. Not when she'd tried to help someone she hoped was a friend.

"I couldn't move it."

Tricia felt her pockets, reality dawning on her. "I didn't give you the key."

"No."

Tricia groaned, then straightened as a man in blue scrubs came toward her. "Gotta go."

"Tricia..."

She closed her phone and exhaled. How typical. Thought she could help someone and her car gets towed. So much for sweeping in and saving the day.

~

NOAH STARED AT THE PHONE. She'd hung up on him. Not that he blamed her... But he missed her voice and its soothing effect. An officer had offered to take him to the vet, but he got nauseous at the thought of it. He could almost smell the strong antiseptic stench from here. No news had to be good news. But he wondered. The police had left after he'd answered their questions. It hadn't taken much. Didn't help that he didn't have anything to say. What could he tell them? He'd barely seen a shadow—then he'd been more focused on the danger to his dog than the fleeing figure. He thought it had been a man, but he couldn't be certain.

He hadn't seen the type of vehicle beyond the impression of a dark sedan. He'd at least noticed a few numbers of the license plate. 018. Big help.

No, the big help of the night had been Tricia, who'd hurried to his side despite the way he'd treated her. Right now he could hear Grandfather's voice lecturing him. It takes a man to humble himself. Think of Christ on that cross. Could anything bring one lower? And there's the Son of God taking on the sin that wasn't His. Extending forgiveness to all who asked. The least you can do is extend the same to those around you. Always consider their needs first.

Grandpa'd talked the talk. And while never as eloquent as Grandpa, Dad had lived with that humble faith.

Humility had always been hard for Noah. He groaned, and his head sank onto his hands. After the way she'd behaved tonight—racing to see if he needed anything, jumping in to take care of Jessie—the last of his doubts had evaporated. The woman who had stepped in to help Jessie in spite of their uneasy past was someone who would make every effort to aid and protect the people she defended. She might not always be successful, but she gave it her all.

Images from the courtroom flashed through his mind. Snapshots of the experience. The mind-numbing realization he'd felt at the time that she wouldn't do anything while other lawyers had ripped his father's reputation to shreds. Maybe he'd asked the wrong question. Maybe the real question revolved around whether she could have stopped the attack.

He turned the thought over in his mind and recoiled at the answer.

He'd spent too much time in a courtroom to claim he didn't understand how it worked. The rules limited attorneys. He hadn't wanted to accept that. No, he'd wanted full vindication. For himself and his father. He ran his fingers through his hair. And if he really wanted to be honest, he'd admit that he'd sought someone to blame. He hadn't saved his father's life. And Tricia hadn't protected his reputation. He'd focused on her to avoid dealing with his own guilt.

Guilt.

The emotion swamped him. Guilt over his father's death. The unjust way he'd treated Tricia. Jessie's accident. Never protecting those he cared about.

The strength drained from him. He'd close his eyes a minute while he waited for Tricia to call. Surely, she'd have news soon. He sank into the couch and leaned his head against the back.

The heat. Noah dragged in a gulp of the stale oxygen from his tank. In. Out. In. Out. He controlled the tempo of his breathing. Flames crackled, the roar overwhelming all other sounds. Static filled his radio.

Graham stood a few feet to his left, searching the room. The systematic search of the building would end soon if the fire didn't respond to the water.

A surge of heat hit him in the chest and knocked him off his feet. Pain seared his knee. He bit his tongue, sensed the metallic taste of blood. He needed to get up. Find his feet. Search for more people. Out, everyone had to get out before the building exploded in flames. The fire lapped across the ceiling, relentless in its hunt for fuel.

Up. He must get up. Now. His mind shouted the command, but his body didn't budge. The fire played games with his mind. It wanted to consume him. Move on to its next victim without his interference.

Graham towered over him. Hauled him up. Pain sliced across Noah's knee. He groaned and winced at the pain.

"You have to help me, you big lug." Grant yanked on his turnout coat. The fire roared as fresh oxygen fueled it. "Come on."

Noah staggered then forced his left leg to accept his weight.

Static cackled in his ear from the radio. "Everybody out now!" The captain's voice boomed. "The building's ready to collapse."

Adrenaline spiked—a heady mix of determination and painkiller.

"We have to hurry, man." Graham pulled him toward the exit.

They reached the door and pounded on the bar. Nothing happened. What? Noah's heart pounded. His breathing raced, loud in his ears.

"Help." A familiar voice whispered across the radio. "A beam's fallen and

got me pinned with one of the civilians." Dad grunted as Noah searched the shadows, desperate to find the man. "I can't move the beam, and the civilian's unconscious."

"Where are you, Pete?" The captain's voice sounded so calm.

"Third floor." He groaned. "Hurry. I'm sharing my air with the kid."

Kid? Noah began to fight Graham. Dad would never abandon a child. Not even if it cost him everything. He put his weight on his foot and groaned.

"A boy. Maybe three or four." Dad's voice seemed to lose strength. How could Noah reach him? He and Graham were on the second floor.

Graham pulled his arm. "Come on, man. We've got to move."

"Dad!"

"Someone else will get him. We've got to get you out." Graham practically carried him toward the next door, punched through it and dragged him down the stairs.

They reached the outside. Graham sagged, features slack as he rested. Noah pushed at the paramedics who rushed toward him. He needed to see Dad, know he was okay. Then the scream combined with sirens...

Noah jerked awake. Sweat covered his face and soaked his shirt. He wiped a hand across his face. Why now? It had been months since his last nightmare. Each time the fire seemed so real. His impotence so paralyzing. The fear so... He gulped. He had to get away from here. He pushed off his couch, staggered to his feet.

His cell phone danced across the coffee table as it rang. He cleared his throat, and popped the phone open. "Brust."

"This is Tricia. I'm downstairs. Can you take me to get my car now?"

"What?" She sounded as exhausted as he felt.

"Can you meet me out in the parking lot?" She yawned. "I need a ride to get my car."

Noah nodded, then realized she couldn't see that. "I called and arranged payment. If we hurry we'll get there before they close."

"That would be good, since I have to work tomorrow."

He hesitated. "How's Jessie?"

"They're holding her overnight for observation. She should be fine in a few weeks."

Tension leeched from his muscles. His dog would be okay. "That's good. Did they give you any details?"

"She didn't break a bone, but she may have a stress fracture. And some ligaments were damaged. I hope you have a first-floor apartment, though."

"Why?" Noah braced himself. Maybe the vet had amputated a limb? She couldn't be paralyzed. She'd moved a bit before Tricia took her. He pulled the phone from his ear. Was it still on? "Tricia?"

"She's in a cast and will be for a while. The vet thinks she'll need help up and down stairs for at least a month."

"Okay." Jessie had some bulk to heft. He'd get his workout schlepping her up and down stairs.

"Hauling a fifty-plus pound dog around sounds challenging." Silence stretched between them as if Tricia were searching for the right words. "But she's alive."

A knowing feeling flooded Noah. Tricia was right. And without Jessie's warning, the night could have ended with him in the hospital or morgue...

But why had someone come after him?

10

Thursday

Tricia stared at the paper through bleary eyes. Her good deed had turned into a night that felt as if it would never end. She'd finally gotten her car back around 11:00 p.m., but hadn't made it home until much later. Thursday morning, and she didn't have the energy to do anything but stay in bed. Unfortunately, that wasn't an option.

The prep work for the Parker trial wouldn't wait. She'd forced herself out of bed and to the office to prepare. Time refused to stand still.

Tricia grabbed the top Parker file and settled in to work. This case had her tied in knots. Trials didn't do that anymore. She wasn't a wet-behind-the-ears attorney. But all she felt when she thought of this one was a ball bouncing in her core.

The image of Andrew staring at her throughout the trial made bile bubble up in her throat.

Peace. She needed it before she threw up in her trash can. Tricia swallowed. *Father, where are You?* She'd felt lost from Him so many times over the years. Why allow the pain in her life? She hadn't felt God in her room the nights Frank invaded or throughout her relationship with Andrew. Her heart knew that God stayed by her side, but sometimes the anger and fear threatened that assurance, making it all but impossible for her to find any kind of peace.

Anger shimmered through her mind, and she fought the urge to let it overwhelm her and overtake her. Burning tingled in her eyes. No! She would not collapse under the emotion. She grabbed a tissue and blew her nose.

"You okay, Tricia?" Sydney slipped into Tricia's office. "Yes." Tricia's voice bit out the word as she turned at the sound. She tried to smile, but couldn't manage it.

Sydney eyed her carefully, every brunette hair in place, makeup perfectly applied to her clear skin. "What's wrong?"

"Nothing."

Sydney snorted. "You'll have to try harder."

"Just a case I didn't want to prosecute."

"Know the kind."

"Yeah. This one's getting to me."

"I'm sorry, but Charlie asked me to grab you for a meeting." Sydney grimaced, her cute nose crinkling across the top. "Something about budgets and policies."

Tricia groaned. That didn't sound any better than working on the Parker case. "Can't you pretend you couldn't find me?"

"Nope. Doesn't strike me as overly honest."

"How about I have to prepare for trial?"

"No, we'll pass notes while you tell me about what had you staring into space. I know there's a story."

Tricia grabbed a notepad and pen and followed Sydney out of her office. "Your imagination's gone haywire."

The meeting drifted around many areas, but seemed to center on something about the coroner duties of the office. Tricia tried not to yawn, while Sydney came to life. She could have all the cause-of-death matters. That was not Tricia's cup of tea. No, she wanted some highly caffeinated cases that took care of the living.

~

TRACES OF SMOKE filled the air. It wasn't the pleasant smoke that came from grilling. This contained hints of something more dangerous and sinister. Noah stared at the back of Weary's head as he studied the fire scene at Jamison's. Had everything inside Caleb's home been affected by the bitter scent? The wind whipped off the lake and through the trees, swirling the smell with it. Noah shrugged deeper into his jacket, pulling the collar up. The calendar read October but it seemed as if winter wanted fall to give way. Too early for that anywhere but Nebraska.

Weary hadn't said a word to him since they'd climbed into the truck. No, the irritating man had turned up the radio—some oldies junk-—all the time pointedly ignoring Noah. Someday Weary would warm to him. Right? Or did this man believe he could alienate everybody and still be effective?

Noah stepped to the side, sheltered a bit by a large oak. Somehow, the tree had avoided the flames. Water dripped from its leaves. Considering the foliage and buildings surrounding the garage, the department had done good work to keep the fire from spreading.

He hoped Caleb realized that.

"Brust. Get over here." The snarl in Weary's words grated against Noah's already shot temper. The late night hadn't done anything for his patience. At least Jessie had gotten proper treatment. Thanks to Tricia.

Noah shuffled to Weary's side. "Yes."

"Getting chippy?"

"Only responding in kind."

Weary laughed, a rich, low sound that rumbled from his gut. "I think I could like you, Brust. You tell it like you see it. A valuable trait in an investigator. Remember to temper it when you interview people of interest, though."

Noah struggled against the sense of whiplash. The man was crazy. Insane. Out of his mind. And Noah had chosen to work with him. No wonder everyone assumed he'd joined the man on the funny farm.

"This is my day off, so if we could get to whatever needs to be done..."

The laugh turned to a snort. "Patience. You've got a lot to learn, young man."

Weary moved toward the back corner of the garage. The wall stood, partially burned, but enough of the structure remained to make out burn patterns.

"Get that camera of yours, and take lots of photos of this wall. What did you get yesterday?"

"Shots of the general scene. Some of activity over by the house."

Weary nodded. "All right. Today we'll focus on the actual fire site." He surveyed the location. "Start with that wall, and we'll see what we find from there. I'm going to get the kit from the truck."

Noah beat Weary to the track, pulled the kit and buckets out for him and grabbed the camera bag. He checked the memory card and batteries, then headed back to the structure. His work boots sloshed through the mud and water. The area would need a good rainstorm and dumpster to clear it of the evidence.

Weary tramped up behind him. "Rain's in tomorrow's forecast. We'll have to get everything we need today."

The two went to work, Weary humming an off-tune song. The wind whistled through the trees as they worked. Noah tried to keep an eye on Weary's movements as he shot photos. The more he watched, the more confused he became. Weary would stoop, kneel and frown, with a look that indicated he'd discovered something, while Noah saw only ruins and ash.

"Come here." Weary waited for Noah, then pointed at a corner along the wall. "See that burn pattern?"

A triangle had formed, starting at the base and flaring up about three feet. Noah eyed it, unsure what he should see.

Weary pulled a pen from his pocket and probed the ashes. He flipped something on top of the pile. "What I thought. See this?" The item he pointed at looked like a charred box about the size of a package of cigarettes.

Noah scratched his head. "Cigarettes?"

"Maybe." Weary sifted through the pile a bit more, scooping a collection of ashes into a bucket. "Grab some photos. This looks like the fire-starter. It's unsophisticated but quite effective. Check this out." He pointed at the container. "It looks like a box of kitchen matches, wrapped in paper, rubber-banded together."

The more Weary explained, the more Noah could see the shell of the materials.

"Pour gasoline or another fuel. Add a cigarette to the package and you have a low-tech timer. Place the device, light the cigarette and walk away." As he talked, Weary scooped several more samples. "It'll smolder and burn down to the matches in about ten minutes. Then you have an instant fire." Weary sealed and labeled the container.

"Sounds easy."

"Yep. Simple and efficient. We'll test the samples to determine if I'm right." His tone indicated that he had no doubt the results would confirm his instincts.

After taking some more samples, they loaded the truck and headed back to the fire station.

Weary hopped out of the truck and grabbed the investigation kit. "Download the photos, and then enjoy the rest of your day off. I'll call you in if anything develops."

Noah nodded, turning over what he'd do. Something nagged him about these fires. He needed to give himself some time to pull the thought from his subconscious. He'd grab his canoe and paddle around Holmes Lake. It'd be cold, but the physical exercise would help him sort through his thoughts and find the missing elements without missing his running partner. He needed to check on Jessie. Make sure she was okay.

Then he needed to talk to Tricia. He owed her an apology. A big one. Would she hear him out? Let him say what he should have said a year earlier?

Maybe too much time had passed. He hoped not. Maybe she still felt a flash of what he did. She had during the trial. No question about it. But that was before he'd made a fool of himself and jumped to all the wrong conclusions. This week she'd acted distant and skittish. He had repair work ahead of him.

Noah couldn't shake the instinct that she might be the arsonist's next target. If his gut was right, then he needed to mend their relationship. Otherwise, Tricia might not let him stay close enough to protect her.

"Anything else you need me to do?"

"Finding out what started the fire is the easy part. The challenge is why. Get with Jamison and his sister and pick their brains. I'll search through old fires for a pattern. Something happened that got this man mad enough to start his own fires."

"You think a previous fire may have triggered it?"

"It's possible." Weary shrugged. "We'll cover all the bases."

Noah nodded, and turned to leave.

When he reached the vacant kitchen, Noah pulled out his cell phone and dialed Caleb Jamison's number. Easier to start there. Jamison answered on the first ring.

"I need to ask you and Tricia some questions."

"I'm working another case. Can this wait?" Caleb's words were rushed.

"How about your mom?"

"I think she's at Tricia's. I don't know how much help she'll be, though. She's determined to bury her head in the sand and ignore the fire."

"She's fortunate it wasn't worse."

"Yep." The muffled sounds in the background intensified.

"Can I get directions to Tricia's?"

Stone-cold silence stretched over the line. Okay, so Jamison didn't like the idea of him talking to his sister. "Weary wants me to ask her some questions. If I don't, he'll have to."

"Lesser of two evils."

Noah laughed at the image. "I guess I am."

"Fine. Here's how you find her." Noah scribbled directions as fast as Caleb threw them out. "And Brust?"

"Yeah?"

"Don't hurt her."

11

Thursday

No light slipped through the windows as Tricia parked in the driveway. She collected her thoughts a minute before getting out of the Miata. The faint scent of meat on the grill wafted into the car from somewhere down the street. Her stomach growled. Time to go in. Fix something for dinner before Mom arrived. Forget about the files she'd brought home for a little while.

The Parker trial wouldn't wait for long, though. Her briefcase bulged with trial prep materials. She'd be ready for Monday, but she'd have to focus and work hard in the interim. Keep dinner short.

For the first time in her career, she wondered if she had the passion to do her job.

Could she separate her past from the case? She didn't see how she could, not when the case revolved around Andrew.

Her stomach cramped, and she pushed open the door. Hiding in her car wouldn't solve a thing. Leaves crinkled as she walked up the sidewalk to her house. She stepped inside and lit her favorite cinnamon-scented candle. Turning on the burner under the teakettle, she listened to her voice mail.

"Tricia, this is Mom. Something's come up with Frank. Can we reschedule? Call me when you get in."

The machine beeped, and Tricia released a breath. A sense of relief washed over her and filled her with guilt at the same time. How could she be so relieved not to have to tiptoe around her mom? Her own mother? The Parker case had forced her to face the truth: she needed to deal with the past. It was time to break its stranglehold on her, and that started with Mom.

Tricia called her mom back and left a message, then fixed a salad while she waited for the water to boil. A little cheese and ham on top of the lettuce bed drizzled with dressing looked perfect. The teakettle whistled, and she poured the boiling water over the tea bag.

Between the sweet scent of cinnamon and the calming aroma of her tea, she felt the stress ease off. She grabbed her Bible and took it to the island with her food. Days had passed since she'd cracked the cover.

Tricia stared at it. Instead of the warmth she usually felt at the thought of approaching her Father, emptiness surrounded her. It seeped into her, almost a physical chill that reached her bones. She hated feeling so empty. But the fires and the Parker case had sapped her strength.

A flush of anger swept through her.

She didn't want to play the victim. Didn't want her past to steal her peace in the present or her hope for the future. But that's exactly what she'd allowed it to do.

She fingered the edges of the book. Lord, I need Your help. I have to get past this bitterness. But I don't know how.

A soft knowing flooded her. He already knew. He understood more than she did the war inside. She opened the Bible to the Psalms, reading one after another. David had expressed every emotion, the good and the ugly to the Lord. And he'd been called a man after God's own heart. Maybe there was hope for her yet.

He would walk with her as she moved out of the mire of her past. He would.

And she was ready to let Him. No matter what the result, she had to do this.

Her cell phone vibrated in her pocket. "Hello?"

A small space filled the air. "Tricia?"

"Yes."

"This is Noah Brust. Could I come over for a minute? I have some questions to ask you about the fire."

Tricia looked at the island, scattered with a mound of clutter. The mess trailed down the hallway into the living room and she didn't want to think about the spectacle in her bathroom.

"I'll bring a pizza or stop at Runza. Whatever you like." His voice strained.

Noah Brust? Pleading for her time?

Tricia opened and closed her mouth. If she sent him for pizza, she'd have a few minutes to get the surface squared away. Ugh. It would take longer than that to regain control of her life and clutter.

"Okay, but I'm not sure how I can help. Why don't you pick up something at Valentino's? I've got Pepsi or sparkling water here."

"Thanks." His voice relaxed at her agreement. "I'll be there in fifteen minutes."

Tricia stared at her phone a minute. He must have already ordered if he thought he'd make it to her house in fifteen minutes with a pizza. And how did he know where she lived, since her phone number was unlisted?

The salad would make a nice side for the pizza. Tricia scooped up a pile of mail and dumped it in the junk drawer before grabbing two plates and setting them on the island. She made a similar sweep through the living room, and then wiped down the bathroom. If only she had time to do things right. As long as he didn't look in any closets or inspect any drawers, her housecleaning would pass muster. Barely.

And why did she want to impress him anyway? He'd done nothing but egg her on since seeing her.

A dull ache filled her heart. Why was it that only the wrong men ever had a lasting interest in her? The ones who wanted to use or hurt her?

She lifted her chin and squared her shoulders. She didn't need a man in her life. Certainly not one as misinformed as Noah. No, she couldn't let his muscular build and rugged features distract her. He'd only hurt her.

All men did.

NOAH WHISTLED as the aroma of Valentino's filled his car. He'd read her like a book. A pizza girl. Toppings, though, had taken some guessing. Who knew what would please a woman like Tricia? Pepperoni? Nah, too dull. Cheese? Too greasy. Ham and pineapple? He grimaced at the thought of the sweet and spicy pizza that sat next to him. What was it with women liking that odd combination? With his luck, Trish would hate it, and he'd have to pretend he wanted it all for himself. All ten slices.

Noah glanced at the directions and turned onto the next street. He slowed to catch the house numbers. In the early dusk, he had to strain to read them.

There. He pulled to a stop in front of a small home. The bungalow had some sort of plant—probably roses—climbing along the porch. Picture-perfect for a woman like Tricia.

The pizza box burned his fingers as he grabbed it and the sack of breadsticks. Hopefully, the gift would negotiate a peace between them. He rang the doorbell and then listened for footsteps. They came quickly, tapping against what must be wood floors. Was she wearing heels at home? She opened the door, and he glanced down. Yep, a wood floor and some kind of heeled shoe on her feet. He looked up at her face. A puzzled expression covered her face.

"Sorry. Checking your floors. And shoes." What a blithering idiot. Time to stop before he said something completely stupid. He held out the pizza. "I hope you like ham and pineapple."

Her face lit up. "I always thought it was a strange combination until I tried it." She inhaled and smiled. "Smells wonderful."

She led him down the hallway, and he took in the home's appearance. An overstuffed navy couch with pillows scattered across its surface, overloaded bookshelves and a small entertainment center filled the living room. A touch of what his grandmother called country evident in the white curtains.

The kitchen was painted a pale yellow. Counters lined two walls, with a small island in the middle. Magazines and papers sat in piles on the countertop, and a salad and plates decorated the island.

"Go ahead and put the pizza there. Would you like some Pepsi?" Tricia bit the corner of her lip.

"Sure. Can't think of the last time I had Pepsi."

"My grandpa's a Pepsi-only kind of guy. Guess I picked up his tastes along the way." She poured a glass then handed it to him. "Go ahead and fill a plate. We'll sit at the table."

Noah followed her gesture. A bistro-style table and chairs sat in the corner of the room. He tossed two slices and a helping of salad onto his plate. They got settled at the table, and she waited while he said grace. She didn't seem surprised, which made him think she remembered their conversations. The ones about his faith forming an important foundation for his life, just as hers did. They had the important things in life in common. And the woman never stopped giving to others. Selflessness defined her.

"So why did you need to see me? Other than needing someone to share a pizza." A strand of hair fell over her eye. He wanted to reach out and move it, see if it felt as silky as it looked, but she tucked it behind her ear in a careless gesture before he could act on the impulse. She looked up and caught him watching her. "What?"

"Tricia, there's something I need to say."

Wariness shadowed her face, as if she were bracing for whatever he would say. This wasn't the reaction he wanted.

"Don't worry. It's nothing serious. At least I hope not." Here he went again, getting all tongue-tied around her. What was it with him tonight? "What I meant is..." He took a deep breath, then gazed into her fearful eyes. "I'm sorry."

"Sorry?"

"Yes. Tricia, I blew it last year. I judged you after the trial and jumped to conclusions, the wrong ones about you. Can you forgive me."

A flash of emotion replaced the fear. Could it be hope?

"I forgive you." The words whispered into the space between them, so soft he almost didn't hear them. It wasn't the reaction he'd hoped for, but it was a start. Then he noted the promise of a smile at the corners of her lips. That was good, right?

Tricia lowered her gaze, and picked at a piece of pizza. "How's Jessie?"

"Okay." Noah shrugged. "I'm relieved she's home, but a second-story apartment isn't the best right now. I have to carry her up and down the stairs. Thanks again for your help last night."

"Glad I could."

"Not everyone would have dropped everything when I called."

"Yes, they would have."

Tricia didn't seem to like the compliment. Her spine stiffened to the point that he could almost hear it crack. "Relax, Trish." He tipped her chin up until she looked him in the eye. Stilled when he saw tears lining her lower lashes. "What's wrong?"

She sniffed and shrugged out of his touch as if burned. "Nothing. I'm fine. Just a long day, and I brought work home."

"Let me help."

Tricia laughed. "You're insane. Nobody wants to work domestic violence."

He nodded. "Maybe. But you have to admit we make quite the team. The dynamic duo ready to put all defendants in jail."

"I think we'd have more success with the fires."

"All right." Noah stood and grabbed another slice of pizza. "Would you like one?" She shook her head and he sat.

"Our arsonist is escalating, and we have to figure out why." Before he comes after you. Noah wanted to say the words, but held his tongue. "What's caused him to be so angry and upset? And why now? We don't have much to go on."

"And I come in how?"

"For some reason he set fire to your mom and your brother's property. Any idea why someone would do that?"

"Because he doesn't like us much." Tricia picked at her salad.

"Then what will keep him from coming after you?"

"I don't know." She took a gulp of Pepsi. "Do you want me to say I'm scared? Fine. I've counted. I know I'm next if the perpetrator has a vendetta against my family." Her voice rose with each word. "But Dani could be next if Caleb's the one they're angry at. And what if the hit-and-run last night was connected?"

The thought pinged through his mind, raising an uncomfortable "what if" he'd toyed with throughout the day. "Maybe. The gasoline can suggests it. But that only complicates the matter. How would I be connected? I'm only one of several fire investigators. Now what?"

"It doesn't make sense. There's nothing my mom has done that would make her a target. She lives a quiet life." Tricia rubbed her eyes and pushed back from the table. "Caleb and his pal Westmont are examining Caleb's cases. We need to explore a different angle."

"I'm not convinced that I'm a target." Noah took a big bite and swallowed. "A fire and a hit-and-run are two different crimes." He held up a hand to stem her protest. "Even with the gasoline can. A lot of people live in that complex."

"But not all of them drive your vehicle."

"True." He smiled as she bulldogged him. "Even if I am a target, it could be an attempt to get me to back off the investigation."

"Maybe you interrupted him before he could start a fire. Or he was investigating."

Noah thought about it, but it didn't sit right. "It's possible, but unlikely. He wouldn't carry the can to sneak around."

Tricia stared at him a moment, then blushed and looked away, scooting her chair back a bit. Noah grinned. He hadn't realized Tricia had moved her chair closer to his. Slowly, cautiously, he inched his chair over next to hers, closing the gap she'd created.

The soft aroma of her perfume wrapped around him. And the look on her face made him want to kiss her. He'd spent so long fighting the urge to be close to her. Now that she'd forgiven him and they'd put the past behind them, perhaps they could stop fighting.

He couldn't explain or understand the way she made him feel. And given their shaky past, he knew he shouldn't rush things. She couldn't think he didn't respect or value her the way she deserved. But ignoring the spark between them hadn't done either of them any good.

He'd always had a weakness for playing with fire.

12

Thursday

Noah's gaze fell to her lips then pulled back up. She felt a tingle surge through her. He wanted to kiss her.

A charge of panic coursed through her. Would he detect her past? How violated she'd been? Most men weren't interested in women like her, not once they knew the truth. It never mattered that she'd had no choice. They cared about what others had done to her. Noah Brust didn't seem like most men, but she'd thought that before and been let down.

Noah leaned in closer, the faint scent of musk aftershave tickling her nose.

Her mind screamed that he was a man, completely unreliable, like the rest. Her heart wanted to argue.

She closed her eyes. Broke the hold his gaze had on her. Felt chilled to the core. "Noah."

He chuckled, a deep, appealing sound. She opened her eyes, expecting to see a wry smile on his face. Instead, Andrew hovered between them, as tangible as if he were standing there. In the flesh. The last man she'd trusted. The last man she'd let betray her. Fear tightened her gut and almost forced her to double over. "I'm sorry."

She stifled a groan. "I'm not feeling well." She hurried from the room and closed the door to her bedroom behind her.

He came to her door and knocked. Concern laced his voice. "Trish? Are you okay? I won't leave unless I know you're okay."

She didn't say anything. What could she say? That she couldn't live with herself? That as much as she longed for true freedom, the past still trapped her? No, the truth wouldn't work. "I'll be okay."

She heard movement on the other side of the door.

"Tricia..." The word trailed off, but she remained silent. She couldn't let him in, risk the hurt. "Okay. Call if you need anything." A shuffling sound penetrated the door, but she didn't hear any retreating footsteps.

Tears slipped down her cheeks, but they had nothing to do with physical pain. No, this pain came purely from the hold Andrew and Frank still had on her. Ten years may have passed, but she still judged every man she met against her ex-boyfriend and her stepfather's low standard.

Tricia swallowed, then tried to find a voice that would convince him to go.

"I'll call tomorrow."

She waited, but didn't hear anything else. He must have taken her words at face value.

Would she ever allow herself to risk? To trust again?

Her hand rubbed her scar, the mark dimpled at her touch. Noah's footsteps retreated down the hall. She waited to hear him close the front door behind him. Watched him leave through the curtains at the bedroom window.

"God, help me." The words ripped from her throat. She screamed at the ceiling. "I don't want to feel this way anymore. Help me break free."

Andrew's image floated through her mind, then morphed into Frank's. She had fought their hold so long. And she was so tired. All she wanted was to live free. But her memories of the past still poisoned all her chances at happiness.

Father, I thought I'd moved past this.

In the silence her thoughts echoed back. No, she hadn't dealt with the past, hadn't allowed herself to dig deeply into the wells of pain she knew existed. Once she dipped her toes in those cesspools, she wasn't she she'd escape. Had she ever confronted her mother with the truth? No. Had she ever told Caleb how much she'd needed him? No. Had she truly turned it over to God? No. She hadn't been willing to hand over her pain if it meant letting go of her anger.

A pulse of rage jolted her. Shouldn't God have protected her? He could have stopped the pain. "Where were You?" The words ripped from her throat.

Tricia grabbed a glass from her bedside table and threw it against the wall. The glass shattered, and cranberry juice flowed down the wall. It pooled at the bottom, a crimson stain against the beige carpet. Tricia stared at the stain, breath coming in fast gallops.

She remained helpless to do anything to stop the pain or the past's assault.

The stain needed to be blotted, sponged up and out of the carpet's threads, but she wouldn't be able to do that anymore than she could do remove her own stains.

Tricia covered her head and sank to the floor. She curled on her side and sobbed. Time stood still as a horrible slideshow played through her mind. Images of Andrew and Frank taking turns tormenting her.

A filthy feeling covered her. How could she think she'd ever be worthy of anyone's love? Men had shown her over and over the fallacy of that hope.

A wail broke through her clamped lips. She tried to suck it back. Tricia Jamison did not lose control. Tricia Jamison fixed other people's problems. Tricia Jamison had fractured into a million pieces.

God, help me. The words formed a desperate plea. She had to know He saw her. That *El Roi* cared about her.

Her sobs returned. Why had He never made His presence known? All she wanted was peace, forgiveness, love.

Pounding shook the front door.

"Tricia? Let me in." A familiar voice?

She lifted her head from the floor, but couldn't move. Her mind had slowed down. Forming a thought took exhausting effort in the aftermath of her fight. Every muscle in her body seemed weighted down. A shroud of grief layered over her.

"Tricia, I'm coming in if you don't open the door."

The door wasn't locked was it? Had Noah locked it when he left? Had he left? Her thoughts were so confused.

The pounding stopped, followed by a crash that sounded like the front door being forced open. She needed to get up. Nobody could see her like this. What if she needed to protect herself?

Heavy footsteps pounded down the hallway. The floor shook under her with each step. She had to claw her way back. Now. She pulled up, then collapsed again. What had happened to her? She didn't fall apart like this. Hadn't in years.

"Tricia!" Caleb entered the room and sank next to her. He pulled her into a hug. "What is wrong?"

"Nothing." The word sounded slurred.

"This is not nothing. I'm taking you to the hospital."

"No!" Her voice pierced the air between them, and Caleb nearly dropped her.

"No? You don't get to make that call, kiddo."

His words lit a fire to the sparks of anger simmering inside her. She pushed against him. "Now you play the hero?"

He stared at her, questions raging in his eyes. "What does that mean?"

"I could have used your protection years ago, but you were off playing the football star. Leaving me to fend for myself." Caleb held her face in his hands, fingers wiping wetness from her cheeks. His eyes locked on hers, a dread filling them. "What are you talking about?"

"You left me with Frank. A monster. The things he did to me."

He closed his eyes and stiffened, as if bracing against a reality he didn't want to see. A nightmare he'd feared. "Frank couldn't... He..." The words trailed off.

"Frank abused me, Caleb. Night after night."

"No, Mom wouldn't have let that happen." His voice was emphatic.

Tricia slumped. She'd expected this reaction, the denial. "It's true."

"Then why didn't you say something?"

"You think it's easy to lead with, 'Hey, our stepfather's abusing me, and Mom won't believe me?' Or how's this, 'The guy from college I thought was so wonderful likes to beat me up.' Would that have made you listen?"

Caleb pulled her closer. "I'm so sorry. I didn't know." Gravel grated his voice.

"But you should have." She took a breath. "And I have to face Andrew on Monday."

Confusion clouded Caleb's face. "Why?"

"I'm the prosecutor on his battery case. Now he's using his wife as a punching bag."

She looked away, and her jaw dropped when she spotted Noah leaning against the doorframe.

~

NOAH SHIFTED HIS WEIGHT. This was not what he'd expected, but he'd been concerned when he'd heard the crash and screaming. That's why he'd called Caleb. But this... this rage and anger. If she hadn't before, she would hate him now. The slackness of her jaw and vacant eyes telegraphed her horror that he'd overheard. If he'd known, he would have walked away. Spared her the embarrassment, but he couldn't move now, not without confirming her worst fears.

"You brought him with you? Why not sell tickets, Caleb?" The pain and shame in Tricia's words pierced him.

Caleb flinched. "He called me. Let me know there was a problem." Noah could sense him searching for words. "I'm glad he called. You needed me here."

"You maybe. I didn't ask for him to see...this." Tricia gestured broadly, hand circling in the air. Then she looked at him, and he could see straight to her soul. To the betrayal vying with fear. No woman should experience what she'd described. And she'd left so much unsaid that he could only imagine. Noah grimaced at the thought.

"What?" Tricia leaned against Caleb the starch draining from her. "Do I disgust you now?"

"No, Tricia. Nothing anyone does to you could make me think less of you." Noah crouched in front of her.

Caleb looked back and forth between them, clearly trying to decide whether to intervene.

"Tricia, look at me." She tucked against Caleb, and Noah felt the sting. "You have to believe I'm not like these other men. I would never hurt you, and I still care for you."

"That's easy to say now. Wait until what you heard settles in." Caleb's shirt muffled her words. He leaned closer to catch them. "I don't want your pity." Tricia's words were hard.

Noah raked his hands through his hair. "And what about nights like this, when it's too much to take? Are you going to ignore it? Push me away?"

She covered her ears.

Caleb caught his gaze. "Thanks for the alert. I've got it from here."

The not-so-subtle boot to his backside. Noah looked at Tricia. If she wanted him to stay, he would, no matter what Caleb said about it. But she wouldn't look at him. Fine, he could take a hint. "Don't forget about the front door. I'm not sure the lock will hold after the hurry to get inside." Caleb nodded, though his attention remained focused on Tricia. Noah felt for his cell phone, and pulled it out to make a call. He might not be allowed to comfort Tricia right now, but he could take care of her door. And pray.

Noah got in his car and started driving home. The only problem was he didn't want to go there. His thoughts were too messed up to allow him to calm down for the night.

He turned toward the fire station. Anything was better than lying in bed, confronted by his thoughts. He needed something physical he could do. Something that didn't require coming up with the right answer. The workout equipment at the station would be the perfect outlet for his pent-up energy and frustration. He couldn't fight the men who'd hurt Tricia, but he could knock around the punching bag and weights. Once he got there, he changed into gym shorts and a T-shirt.

"What's brought you here on your night off?" Graham stared at him from a neon orange lawn chair.

"Ready to pound you at weightlifting."

Graham grinned, probably remembering the last time Noah had issued a challenge like that. Graham had ended up $20 richer while Noah suffered through a pulled muscle. Noah grinned—the pain of competition. That he could handle.

In minutes Noah sweated as he bench-pressed weights. Graham stood over him ready to help.. .as if he'd need it.

"Want to talk about what's on your mind?"

"No."

Graham looked at him, one eyebrow raised. "No?"

"You heard me."

"All right. Let's make you work then."

"Yeah." Noah strained against the weight. All problems should be solved like this. Apply steady pressure and some sweat equity. Change reality by action.

His thoughts wandered back to Tricia. If only he could lift away her past and pain as easily.

~

Caleb handed Tricia a tissue. She shuddered and wiped her face. She felt exposed, and moved away from him. It had been easy to lean on him when she wanted his help getting rid of Noah. But they were alone now, and her confessions had had time to sink in. How would he handle them? She wanted to believe he'd protect her, but could she trust him not to push away?

"Why didn't you tell me Noah was here?"

Caleb stared at her. "That's what you're concerned about? Maybe I need to talk to him, determine his intentions."

"I am twenty-nine years old and don't need you vetting guys for me."

"Not vetting. Just trying to protect you. The way I should have done before." Caleb crossed his arms. "Why didn't you come to me, Tricia? I would have tried to stop it."

"Caleb, you've changed a lot since you became a Christian. Back then, life was all you and football."

"I'm sorry."

Tricia nodded. "I know."

"What do we do now?"

That question stymied Tricia. The abuse she'd undergone had dominated her life for years. She knew the correct response: Forgive and move on. But she wasn't sure she knew how.

Caleb wiped a lingering tear off Tricia's cheek. "I'm sorry I didn't stop this. That I didn't notice what happened. That I didn't protect you and you suffered alone. Will you forgive me?"

Fresh tears coursed down Tricia's cheeks. How she had longed to hear those words. But now she didn't know how to handle them. She wanted to forgive, but the pain was wound into the fiber of who she'd become.

She took a deep breath and made a decision. "I forgive you, Caleb."

With those words, a release came in her core. The pain remained, but an edge disappeared. The anger relaxed its hold. "I keep thinking I should have stopped it somehow."

Caleb pulled her close. "What do you mean?"

"Somehow I must have done something to let these men think they could use me."

"Tricia, you didn't do anything wrong. Or anything to deserve the way they treated you."

She wanted to believe him. Had told herself the same things, but the words had never settled into her heart.

"Look at me."

Slowly she raised her gaze to his.

"You are a precious child of God. You are His treasure, and nothing will change that. And somewhere out there is a man who will treat you like that treasure. Until you find him, don't settle for less. You are too valuable."

The words didn't fully soak into her heart, but they brought some hope.

Tricia clung to the feeling. Maybe now some healing could begin.

Then her thoughts turned to Noah. Did he mean what he'd said? Did he truly care for her?

Or would she never hear from him again?

13

F*riday*

"Let's pack up and move to California." Tricia's cell phone sang and danced across her bedside table in time to the wake-up alarm. She groaned and threw an arm over her eyes, but didn't feel the same dread she had for the past week at the start of each new day. After last night, it seemed as if part of her past and its burden had evaporated. No, transferred to Caleb's shoulders, thanks to the way he'd comforted her after Noah left.

Noah.

She sank deeper under the covers. Murky memories of last night's collapse ran through her mind. She pulled the pillow over her head, trying to block out her complete and utter vulnerability. Noah knew everything. And what she hadn't said, he'd probably guessed.

The throbbing of a headache pulsed. Tricia rubbed at it. If the pain was any indication, this could be an extremely long day. The freedom she'd experienced after Caleb left lingered at the edges of her mind. She clung to it. Three days until Monday, and she hadn't finished her Parker trial prep yet. The drumbeat in her head accelerated. She owed it to Linda to do everything in her power to put Andrew behind bars. Three days. She'd need every moment.

Since she didn't have to go to court, she pulled on a simple wool sheath and jacket. Tricia knew she should stop, make some oatmeal, spend time in her devotions, but she didn't have time.

She should be stronger. She'd spent a lifetime loving God, yet she couldn't move beyond her past. Maybe last night had started the process. How she hoped so. Tricia sat on the edge of her bed. She couldn't head into the day without begging God to go with her.

Father, help me move forward. I don't want to stay in the mire of the past. Your Word promises You have more for me. Help me move into whatever You have for me now. First, could You help me get past the Parker trial? Give me the wisdom to do everything I need to before the trial. Not with a purpose of vengeance against Andrew, but for the sake of his wife.

Tricia stood and headed to the kitchen. There she grabbed a Kind bar and ran to her car. By the time she reached her office, she'd relaxed, her mind focused and clear. The stack of files waited, and she tackled them with determination. Her pen flew over a notepad as she made notes for questions for the witnesses.

"Tricia, call on line one."

Tricia shook her head to clear it, and picked up the phone. "Tricia Jamison."

"Hey." Noah's rich tones turned her stomach to mush. She settled back in her chair and pivoted toward the wall. Heat flushed her face at the idea of what he must think. She wasn't ready for this conversation. Her heart reacted to the sound of his voice alerting her she hadn't driven him away after all...and didn't want to.

"I...I didn't expect to hear from you today."

"Do you have time for lunch? I could meet you anywhere you like."

"I don't know what to say." Tricia bit her lip. She always spent her time with men in a state of constant tension, waiting for them to realize the truth about her. But Noah *knew* the truth, and he still wanted to see her. The freedom, the hope she'd felt at Caleb's words the night before settled a little deeper, a little stronger in her heart.

"I still want to spend time with you, Tricia. Nothing you said last night changes that."

His words warmed her. She wanted to spend time with him, too. But today wasn't the day. She had too much pretrial work. "Noah, I'll have to get back to you. Today doesn't look good with the trial on Monday."

"Andrew's case?"

"Yes, but I can't talk about that now."

"Can I call you later?"

Tricia's old instincts told her to say no. She had to protect herself. Make some kind of excuse. But she wouldn't let those old instincts run her life a moment longer. "Yes. I'd like that." The words surprised her as they slipped past her resolve. At the same time they delighted her.

"Me, too." Noah's voice held a smile. "I'll talk to you later. Let me know if you need anything, okay?"

"All right."

"Good luck with the preparations."

Tricia stared at the phone a moment, then hung up. A surge of energy pulsed through her, and she turned back to the pile of files. Time to dive in before Linda came in for her trial prep. She'd be ready to tackle Andrew Parker and her past on Monday. It didn't matter that she didn't have a choice. Maybe that's what she'd needed all along. Something to force her to confront the pain.

~

NOAH CARRIED Jessie down the stairs one more time. He hadn't expected this to form part of her recuperation plan. He lowered her to the ground. She whined. "Sorry, Jessie. Do your business."

Big brown eyes stared at him, sorrow tingeing them as if asking why he didn't like her anymore. Too bad she couldn't understand how guilty he felt already. He hadn't even protected his dog a few nights ago. So far police hadn't narrowed down any suspects. Too many license plates with 018 and too few other details to make much progress, so they leaned toward accident. He didn't believe it. Not when reasonable, innocent people would have stopped.

If he couldn't keep his dog from getting hit or save his father, how did he think he could protect Tricia? Talk about pride.

He couldn't protect anyone. It didn't matter that he'd signed up as a firefighter to do exactly that. Reality painted a very different picture. One filled with his ineptness. One he did not like.

Noah shook his head. Tried to clear the thoughts. This wasn't going anywhere. He picked up Jessie and climbed the steps, then entered the apartment. He'd feel more focused and sure of his next steps after work. After a shower, he headed to the fire station. Time to focus on something he could control. Doing a great job in his calling.

When he walked into the kitchen, a group stood leaning against the counters. "What's up?"

Bob glanced at him and away. "It's been a busy week."

Noah frowned. "What do you mean?"

"What he means is while you've been off investigating fires we've already put out, we've had to fight a bunch of fires." Graham crossed his arms, dark smudges under his eyes.

"More than usual?"

Bob groaned. "Brush fires. Small buildings. Some look accidental. Some natural causes. Others we're not sure."

"But lots of little fires."

Graham nodded.

Noah rubbed his neck, mind spinning. "Any of them look related?"

"Don't play fire investigator now, Noah." Bob grimaced at him, hostility radiating from him. He turned and stalked out of the room, bumping into Noah as he passed.

"What's gotten into him?"

"Don't forget he wanted to be an investigator, but didn't last. Weary wore him down."

That's right. Another one of Weary's casualties. And another reason Noah had to make this work. He didn't want to turn bitter over a lost chance.

His knee twanged, reminding him that he couldn't blow this chance.

No, and he couldn't ruin this opportunity with Tricia, either. The thought of the sadness hidden in her eyes made him want to shelter her.

He wished he could rewind time and undo his actions from a year ago. Somehow he'd find a way to show her that she could depend on him. That he was worthy of her trust. And maybe one day her love.

Saturday

Tricia decided she should see Caleb. He'd called to check on her yesterday, but she hadn't seen him face-to-face since her startling revelation. Protective big brother needed to see with his own eyes she was okay. Well...getting there.

Maybe he could come for dinner and she could cook something simple for them. She dialed his number and waited for him to pick up.

"Hey, Trish."

"How about coming over for supper tonight?"

"Only if I can bring Westmont and boxes of files."

"What kind of files?"

"We've been slogging through my case files and still have boxes to go."

Simple it was then. "I'll order the pizza and see if Dani can join us."

"Great. We'll be over around six." A siren sounded in the background. "Gotta run. See you tonight."

Tricia hung up the phone. Not exactly how she would have planned to spend the evening, but at least he'd see she was okay.

What to do with the rest of her day? She could head to campus and watch all the fans stream to the stadium for the afternoon's football game. She loved how the stadium was the third largest city in the state on football Saturday's. Or she could go to the mall and wander aimlessly. No, she'd rather do something that mattered. That left work and the trial.

Half an hour later she drove past the state capitol where it pierced the sky, and found a parking spot down J Street closer to Tenth and the City-County Building. She stumbled out of her Miata into the chilled October air. Leaves crunched under her feet, and she hurried through the doors out of the cold.

She slipped into her office and saw the light blinking on her phone. She walked to her desk and sat before hitting the button to listen to the message.

"Hi, Tricia. This is Barb from the victim's advocate's office. It's Friday at six o'clock, and I just got off the phone with Linda Parker. She says she can't testify Monday, but won't say why. I couldn't determine what's changed, but wanted to let you know as soon as I could. Maybe you can change her mind."

What? Everything had been fine when Linda left her office at four. What could Andrew have done to her in the two hours before Barb's call? Tricia leaned back against the chair. What could she do now? It was Saturday late morning. Odds were slim that she could find opposing counsel to ask for a continuance. Odds were even slimmer that he'd agree after she fought him on a continuance last week. And did she really want one?

The thought of restarting this case in another month or two filled her with dread. If Andrew was threatening Linda, then waiting wouldn't make things better. No, she'd get Linda on the phone. Find out what had changed and convince her that it wouldn't become easier if she waited. Remind her that Andrew wouldn't change.

Tricia grabbed the file with Linda's statement and contact info. Pulling a notebook toward her, she dialed the number.

"Hello?" The deep, rich voice made Tricia's heart stop. She tumbled back in time to the days they were an item.

"Is Linda there?" She struggled to keep her voice steady and calm.

"No." Andrew hesitated a moment. "Can I take a message?"

"I'll try later." Tricia hung up and released the phone as if it had singed her trembling fingers. Polka dots spotted her vision, and she sucked in a deep breath. If a short, inane conversation turned her into a mess, how would she handle Andrew at the trial on Monday? if there were a trial.

14

Saturday

Noah's shift came to an end, and he gladly headed home. Mrs. Rivers had called his cell phone several times about a barking, moaning Jessie. His neighbor had a good heart, but she couldn't do anything to help Jessie, an answer she didn't like. At all. She'd used her key to try to drag Jessie out, but that had ended in disaster. He needed to get home and let Jessie out.

Jessie needed help he couldn't give her when he was at work. And Mrs. Rivers couldn't get her up and down the stairs the way she usually did while he was at work. Maybe he needed to kennel her until her leg healed. He hated the thought of her stuck in a place like that, but most of his friends either didn't want a big dog visiting or lived in apartments, too.

He had to do something. Jessie needed more than the status quo.

His phone vibrated against his hip and he clicked the Bluetooth button to take it. "Brust."

"Hey, this is Caleb Jamison."

Noah stifled a sigh. Caleb wasn't the Jamison he'd wanted to talk to. "What's up?"

"I'm getting ready to have a file review party. How'd you like to participate?"

The police letting a firefighter in? "Sure. What are we looking for?"

"A dead file that might lead to whoever set the fires."

"Couldn't you come up with something easier?"

"Any better thoughts?" Caleb's voice held an edge to it.

"No. Why now?"

"It's the weekend. I'd like to use the time to look at files."

Noah nodded. Getting a step ahead was ideal. "When and where?"

"Tricia's in half an hour."

"I have to run home first and let my dog out."

"Bring her with you. Tricia's got a fenced yard." Noah hesitated, which Caleb must have taken for uncertainty. "She won't mind."

"Okay." He drew the word out and ended the conversation. Once home, he ran through the shower and changed. Jessie stayed close to him, and he tripped over her as he tried to pull on his jeans.

"Come on, girl. You need the break." He carried Jessie down the stairs and hoped Tricia would forgive him. If she didn't, he'd blame it on Caleb.

Twenty minutes later, Jessie hobbled around Tricia's backyard. She turned a circle and settled underneath a half-dressed maple tree. A soft smile played on Tricia's lips. "She's made herself at home."

"I hope it's all right." Noah crossed his arms in the chilled air. Some hardy soul had fired up a grill in the neighborhood if his nose identified the scent correctly. His stomach grumbled. He should have taken the five minutes and grabbed an energy bar at home or grabbed a Runza at the closest franchise.

Tricia gestured toward Jessie. "Glad you brought her. The yard needs a dog, but I haven't done more than dog-sit Dani's occasionally. A dog seems like...a big responsibility." She shrugged, a droop to her shoulders. "Maybe when life feels more settled."

Caleb walked up behind Tricia and slung an arm around her shoulders. "You'll get there soon."

At his words Tricia smiled. Noah was surprised to realize that he felt unsettled and envious. He wanted to be the one who brought a smile that size and genuine to Tricia's face.

"So where are those files?" He didn't know how he could contribute to the search, but he had to refocus Tricia off Caleb.

"I brought three boxes with me. Todd Westmont's bringing two more in an hour." Caleb led the way back inside.

Noah gulped. Five boxes of files? They'd expect him to keep up. Pull his weight. Was now the time to tell them he had difficulty reading? Or should he wing it? See how hard the files were?

Tricia looked at him with a funny expression. "Are you okay?"

"Um, yeah. Didn't realize there'd be that many."

"Caleb's spent a career making enemies."

"Not that you're any better." Caleb bumped her shoulder.

"Maybe not. But they're usually angrier at the police who catch them."

Noah laughed. "You can have your one-upmanship on who's hated more than the other. I want to know where the food is."

"Leading with your stomach?" Tricia crinkled her nose at him.

"Absolutely. Rumor has it that's what men do."

Caleb laughed and led the way into the house. "The Valentino's man should be here in a few minutes. Pizza and lasagna work?"

Noah licked his lips and rubbed his stomach. "Absolutely. Much better than the manwich I would have fixed. Only thing better are Runza onion rings."

Caleb shook his head. "Give me their fries any day."

"Enough about the food." Tricia shook her head as she glanced between them. "Let's get to work. I've still got trial prep to finish."

Noah sobered and studied her. She looked strained around the edges. Had something new happened to upset her?

The front door bounced open, and Dani Richards breezed in. He took in her perfect package—emerald eyes and blond hair—but quickly turned back to Tricia. Caleb could have the blonde look. Noah would take Tricia's rich brown hair and cinnamon eyes any day.

Dani hurried to Caleb and gave him a kiss that he deepened.

Noah looked away and found Tricia's gaze. She looked as uncomfortable as he felt.

"Okay, you guys." Tricia's voice teased, and the two pulled apart. "Let's get to work." Boxes lined Tricia's dining room table. "Caleb and I each have a box, Noah. Do you want your own, or do you want to help us track what we learn?"

Noah shrugged as relief coursed through him. "I'll do whatever you need."

"Grab a handful of files. You and Dani can share the box."

Soon they were sprawled around the living space. Caleb had his box on the coffee table and huddled over it, looking slightly ridiculous on the feminine couch as he slowly flipped through each file. Dani cuddled next to him with a small pile in her lap. She read each file intently as if they contained the secrets of the universe. Tricia had sprawled on the floor with the files stacked in front of her. She flipped through each as if knowing exactly what she was looking for. Within a couple minutes of opening a file, she'd deposit it to her left and grab the next one.

Noah settled at the table and picked up his first file. Jordan Matthews. Looked like the guy had been a suspect in an armed robbery. While he understood most of the file, he didn't understand the goal. "What exactly are we looking for?"

"You'll know it when you see it." Caleb flipped through his file.

Tricia groaned. 'Tell me he didn't really say that."

Dani sidled closer to Caleb. "My fiancé is so articulate."

Noah tossed the file to the side. "It's not very helpful for the uninitiated." He stood up. "Anyone else need a drink?" He took the few steps to the galley kitchen and grabbed a glass out of the rack in the sink. Filling it with water, he guzzled it before marching back. He'd find something to add to the hunt. Noah stopped when he reached the doorway.

"...a complete waste of time." Tricia sounded upset.

"Do you have any better ideas?" Caleb had shifted to the floor in front of Tricia, a pile of files beside him.

Tricia shrugged. "I think we need to think more broadly. You're assuming you're the true target. I don't think that explains Mom's house or the incident at Noah's apartment."

Dani eased from the couch to sit on the floor next to Caleb. "Tricia's got a point."

Noah stood watching Tricia and could feel the tension rolling off her.

The doorbell rang, and they all looked up. Noah moved to open the door. "I'll get the pizza."

"No, I'll take care of it." Caleb stood and then brushed him aside on the way to the door.

"He must have had a rough day." Dani shook her head. "This case and the lack of answers really bother him."

Noah nodded, but watched Tricia grab plates and silverware. And Caleb's insistence that the investigation be done his way wasn't helping her mood. Tears hovered at the edge of her lashes. He reached up to brush them away, and stilled when the air charged between them. She must have noticed it, too, because she stepped away from him. "Don't do that, Tricia."

She didn't say anything, but also didn't retreat farther. Caleb walked through the living room to the kitchen with the pizza and pasta. Noah's stomach danced at the thought of Valentino's. Caleb opened the box and grabbed a slice while Dani and Tricia took lasagna.

A knock at the door had Dani out of her chair to open it. "Hey, Westmont."

"How's my favorite journalist?"

"Well." She held the door for him. "Go ahead and put those on Tricia's table."

Tricia grabbed her plate and scooted back from the table, staring at the boxes. "How long are you leaving them, Caleb?"

"The weekend. We'll have to take them back Monday."

"We're focusing on the wrong area."

Westmont put a hand on Caleb's arm. "Why?"

"We're assuming Caleb was the target all along." Tricia walked to the boxes and flipped through the files. "We won't find the suspect here."

"It could be random." Noah took a bite of pizza and thought about all the little calls the guys complained about. "There's been a lot of fire activity lately. Small fires, but damaging, too."

"So Mom and you could be part of that." Tricia rubbed her arms. "There must be some warning that something will happen. We need to anticipate where, and then we can catch him in the act."

"I know." Caleb snapped, then sighed. "I know." His words were quieter this time.

Noah leaned against the wall. "What's this really about, Jamison?"

Caleb looked at him, then at Westmont. "I can't risk anything happening to either of these women. Right now we're walking blind. The risk is completely unpredictable. Maybe we'll get a warning. Maybe we won't. Even if we do, he's been subtle so far. We won't know what or who he's targeted. He's still out there. And I have to find him before he does anything else."

"Then you three go through these boxes. See what you can find." Tricia slid next to Noah. "We're going to look at this from a different angle." She grabbed the empty plates and stacked them.

"What angle is that?" Noah whispered in her ear.

"I'm not sure. But it's got to be more effective than this."

15

Saturday

Tricia hoped Noah would follow her to the kitchen...and that Caleb wouldn't. Her brother had fully adopted his protector mode and couldn't distance himself enough from the situation to view things objectively. Dani could calm him better than Tricia. But Dani would need time alone with Caleb to make that happen.

Of course, that meant she would be alone with Noah. The thought almost brought a smile.

She groaned. How could her thoughts go that direction? They still had so many obstacles ahead of them. Finding the arsonist. Handling the Parker trial. Recementing her trust in God. She didn't have time to worry about romance.

Tricia eased out the back door and sat down on the stoop. Jessie limped to her, tongue lolling to the side. "Like the freedom?" She pulled the sleeves of her sweatshirt over her fingers against the cold and scratched behind Jessie's ears. Jessie leaned in to her touch, so she kept rubbing, laughing as she did. "You're a beggar, aren't you?"

"The worst kind." Noah leaned against the door. He smiled at her, then eased next to her on the step. "So what's your grand plan?"

Tricia kept her gaze on the dog. What censure must fill his gaze, regardless of the soft tone in his voice. "I should go to work and finish preparing for Monday's trial." She plopped her elbows on her knees and cupped her chin in her hands. "If there is a trial."

Noah bumped her shoulder with his and a shiver raced up her spine. "Why wouldn't there be?"

"My key witness is unavailable, and I got a message this morning that she's decided not to testify. The case falls apart without her." With no time left to fix it. A dull pounding started behind her temples. She needed more Tylenol.

"So let's focus there." He held up his hands as she started to protest. "It's the more immediate problem. There's nothing we can do about the fires right now at—" he looked at his watch "—7:00 p.m. on a Saturday evening. However, we might make a difference in your trial. I've seen how hard you work to make your cases come together. What would stop the witness from testifying?"

"Other than her husband?" Tricia shrugged. "Linda's a stay-at-home mom. Without him, she doesn't have a place to live or a way to put groceries on the table."

"You can explain alternatives to her."

"I could. I have. She's panicked before, and I've talked her down. But I haven't reached her today. Andrew, he's..." She sighed. "It's hard to describe the kind of hold he exercises. But I've experienced it."

"This is the guy you dated?" At her nod, Noah's face stilled. "No wonder this trial is different. Tell her about it. Explain that you understand."

At the thought, she wiped sweaty palms against her jeans and licked her lips. Didn't he understand this wasn't the kind of information you shared with a client? She could imagine how it would go. *Hi, Linda. This is Tricia Jamison, the prosecutor assigned to your husband's case. By the way, have I mentioned that he and I dated and he abused me? I know what you're going through.* Yep, Linda would be thrilled to learn her attorney had experienced the same abuse at her husband's hands but had done nothing.

"Not a good idea." The words sounded blunt and pointed, even to her ears. "That's not what Linda wants to hear."

"What if you're wrong? What if that's exactly what she needs to hear? That she's not alone? That you understand what she's going through? The choices she has to make?"

Tricia stopped. What if he was right? "Maybe. I'll think about it."

"That's all I ask." Noah leaned back on his elbows, long legs sticking out, calm patience on his strong features.

The rising moon reflected off her neighbor's windows. Tricia tipped back to watch it. Dusk lowered with the hint of stars dotting the velvet sky. The gathering night didn't threaten her with Noah next to her.

Tricia pulled her cell phone out. "I'll try Linda again. I'm ready if she sticks. Then we need to come up with a theory about the fires."

Noah chuckled. "You don't give up, do you?"

"Nope. Never." She pulled up Linda's number and waited for the call to connect. "Hello. Is Linda home?" She slowly hung up. "I guess she's out tonight, too." She whispered a quick prayer for Linda's protection.

~

NOAH WATCHED Tricia from the corner of his eye. She was wound as tight as he'd ever seen her. The stress of this trial and trying to find the arsonist had her on edge, but now he understood what made this trial more stressful even than the Lincoln Life fire.

Too bad he didn't have any ideas on how to help her. He'd proven he didn't understand trials a year ago. The thought bubbled up in his mind. What if...?

"What?"

He startled and looked at Tricia. "Hmm?"

"You might as well spill it. You had some kind of *aha* thought." She shivered, and he put an arm around her shoulders. She tensed, but didn't move away.

"Let's get you inside. I need to think about it a bit more, but I think you might be right."

"You can't tease me like that."

He opened the door and let her through. It made sense. But only if Tricia were the next target and Jessie's accident hadn't been random. He wasn't sure about the second and didn't want to believe the first. Not without more evidence.

Nope, better to keep his thought to himself a bit longer. Get the focus back on her trial while he built his theory, tested it for soundness.

"What other witnesses can you call if Linda really doesn't want to testify?"

Tricia rattled off a couple of names.

"Will that be enough?"

"No. That's the challenge with domestic violence cases. Too many victims change their minds before trial. You can understand why, but it doesn't make it easy to build a case. The jury wants to hear the victim. And defense counsel can make things very difficult without that testimony. It's very easy to raise a reasonable doubt in the jury's mind."

"So get those other witnesses on the phone. Prep them and keep trying Linda."

"I think I will." Tricia wrinkled her nose at him. "Didn't know you were an attorney wannabe."

"I didn't either." He'd play the role again if she'd smile.

Caleb stuck his head in the kitchen. "We're calling it a night."

"I'm making him take me out for dessert. He's worked me to the bone," Dani piped up.

Tricia smirked. "Better make it the Green Gateau, Caleb, after making her get paper cuts for you."

In minutes Caleb and Dani had disappeared, holding hands like high school sweethearts, Westmont a step behind them. Tricia led Noah to the now empty living room. He sank into an oversize chair across from the flowered couch. He might not get out of the chair. "What now?"

Tricia curled up with her feet beneath her on the couch. She relaxed as she settled back. "I'm going to head to bed. Clear my head before I do more prep tomorrow."

"Will you go to church?"

"Of course." She smiled sweetly. "So what were you going to tell me out there? You didn't think I'd forget." She looked adorable, with a dimple appearing on her chin. He got the sense that she wouldn't let it drop until he told her.

"I'll fill you in after I do some checking." He stifled a yawn, his shift catching up with him. "I've got to head home and get some rest."

The dimple disappeared, along with the smile. "Would you mind leaving Jessie here?"

"You mean I don't have to carry her up and down the stairs? Sounds like a plan to me. I'll bring her food by tomorrow."

"Thanks." She looked around the room. "I usually feel at peace here. This is my escape from everything. Tonight it feels like Caleb's brought everything to rest here."

He leaned forward and grabbed her hands. "Call if you don't feel safe."

She slipped away from his grasp. "Don't worry, I'll let you get your beauty rest."

"That's not what I'm worried about." He wandered through the kitchen to the back door. "Come here, Jessie." The dog struggled up the couple of steps, but she made it. Staying here was a much better solution than a kennel. Jessie'd love spending time in a yard. "Good night, girl. Be good."

Jessie's ears tipped and her head cocked at an angle as if she understood his words.

Tricia leaned against the doorjamb, watching. "I'll take good care of her."

"I know." He followed her to the door.

She reached for the knob then paused. Their gazes locked, and he could feel the energy pulsing between them. The air almost felt electric. Recognition flashed in her eyes. She looked down, breaking the connection, and blushed.

Noah let the moment slide away. He'd give her all the time she needed. She was worth it. "See you tomorrow."

"Tomorrow." Her voice barely reached his ears, soft as a butterfly's wings.

Instead of heading home, he drove by the Lincoln Life building. He parked his truck across the street from the structure. According to the papers, the exterior construction would be complete in another week or so. A crane remained in one corner of the yard, pointing to the area yet to be finished.

The edges of the building faded as his mind saw the chaos of the fire. It had seemed like any other out-of-control blaze. The restrained chaos of many responders. The systematic but hurried search for survivors. The discovery that some doors were faulty and they'd have to find alternative exits, wasting precious seconds they didn't have.

Could it be that the current fires somehow tied into that one? The theory seemed far-fetched.

And if his theory held water, how to prove it? How to narrow down suspects? He climbed out of his pickup and pushed his hands deep in his pockets. It wasn't any easier to look at from across the street.

He still detoured around the location rather than face his memories and guilt head-on.

If he'd only moved faster, hadn't been distracted by the panicked calls over the radio. Maybe then he could have found a way to reach his dad. Demonstrated he'd become a firefighter worthy of his father's legacy, someone as capable of saving others as the man he'd always admired.

Noah hung his head, weighted by the fresh wave of grief that rolled over him. The fire might be in the past, but there weren't many days that he didn't miss his father. The chance to tell him about a success. Or ask him about a problem he'd encountered on the scene. His dad would have known how to make the most of his shot at fire investigation. Probably would have known Weary, too.

Instead, he'd been left to imagine what his father would say if he were here to speak.

If there were a link, he wanted to find it. Before more harm came.

This had to stop. Now.

~

SUNDAY MORNING TRICIA awakened when her phone rang. She groped for the phone on her bedside table. "Hello?"

"Tricia?" A woman's muted voice quivered.

"Yes?"

"This is Linda Parker."

Tricia bolted upright in bed. "Linda, can we meet today?"

"My son has a soccer game at 3:00 p.m."

"Will Andrew be there?"

"No. He never bothers to come."

Linda gave her directions and told Tricia where to look for her. The fear in her voice carried through clearly from her whispered tone to her quick words. What had Andrew done to her? Tricia didn't know if she could handle the answer. The concern stayed with her through a quick breakfast and the church service. Even during praise and worship she couldn't forget Linda. Instead, she prayed for strength and protection for the woman and her sons. And the wisdom to know what to say.

A few minutes before three o'clock, Tricia pulled her car into the school parking lot and watched the families run to the large field next to the school where someone had set up the goals. At one time she'd imagined spending weekends at events like this. Then Andrew had inflicted his damage. Maybe it was time to resurrect that dream. Time to risk again.

Before the thought could germinate, she stepped from her Miata and followed a family to the camping chairs lining the field. She shielded her eyes as she searched for Linda.

The woman stood at the end by herself while a boy played in the grass at her feet.

Tricia walked over to join her. "Hi, Linda."

The woman started, a shadow passing over her face. She nodded, then clutched the jacket around her neck.

"Are you okay?" Tricia wanted to pull her hand back, see if she hid fresh bruises. Andrew would be smart enough not to hit her face the weekend before the trial, but that didn't mean he'd show restraint in places where the marks wouldn't show.

"I don't know if I can testify tomorrow." The words whispered into the space between them. "Is there any way to convict him without me?"

"It's possible, but unlikely." Tricia took a deep breath. "What's changed since Friday?"

"You wouldn't understand." Defiance outlined Linda's stiff body and the hard set to her jaw. "You've never been stupid enough to fall in love with someone like Andrew."

"You'd be surprised how much I do understand." Could she really do this? Looking at Linda, she knew Noah was right. She needed to share her past with this woman. "Linda, I know exactly what Andrew is like, because we dated in college." Tricia pushed her hair away from her face. "See this scar?"

Linda turned to look at her and reached toward it. She stopped short of actually touching Tricia. "Did he...?"

Tricia nodded. "He did. I thought he was my knight in shining armor. That he would sweep me away from a life I didn't like and take me to a castle where he would protect me. Instead, he swept me into a dungeon of control and fear."

Tricia paused. Could she really tell Linda everything? "I know how demanding he can be. How he can take everything from you. I wish I had stood up to him back then. Maybe I could have stopped him before he found you." Linda opened her mouth, but Tricia held up her hand. "Let me finish. I didn't stop him then, but we can do that tomorrow."

"What if we lose?" Linda's voice had a tremor and a shadow crossed her face. Tricia imagined her concerns. What would happen to the boys? To her?

"Then we'll get you and the boys to a safe place. But I promise I will do everything in my power to expose him for the man he is." How she prayed she could keep that promise.

Hope flickered as Linda searched Tricia's face. "Why didn't you tell me before?"

"Because I'm still coming to grips with that part of my past. Do you want me to find another attorney to handle the trial?" Tricia held her breath. It would be tough, but someone like Sydney might take the case through to the end.

"No. You're the one fighting for me." Linda shrugged. "Besides, I trust you and want you to stay. I'll do this if you're the one asking the questions."

"Thank you." Tricia hugged Linda, intending to give strength but surprised to receive it instead. "I'll see you in the morning at court."

Tricia returned to her car, relieved to have told Linda her story. In doing so, she felt a new freedom from the past. It was as if pulling it into the light caused it to lose some of its power.

One crisis averted. Now to figure out who had targeted her family.

16

M*onday*

Quiet conversation filled the courtroom as Tricia set up her files and organized her exhibits. She felt flushed as she rushed to prepare for jury selection.

Andrew's presence from his seat at the adjoining defense table blazed in her consciousness.

Every nerve and sense seemed attuned to him. He looked good, and she hated that. Shouldn't his outside reflect the depravity that lurked within?

Tricia looked behind her and caught Sydney walking through the door. Sydney had volunteered to come watch for Linda to make sure neither Andrew nor Earl intercepted her.

Sydney slipped next to her at the table. "Morning."

Tricia swallowed hard against the block in her throat. "Good morning."

"You okay?"

"Sure." Tricia stacked the files in front of her. "Just another day at the office."

Sydney rolled her eyes. "Right. Linda is waiting in the back row."

"Thanks." Tricia kept her gaze on the front of the courtroom where the judge's bench rose above everyone else. Time to focus on the trial. Try to push past the reality of who she was prosecuting. Fat chance of that happening, but she'd fight for Linda and her boys. That's where she needed to place her focus.

"All rise."

Everyone in the courtroom stood with the bailiff as Judge Sinclair swept into the room, her robes flowing behind her. She settled into her chair. "You may be seated." She flipped through her notes then turned her attention to the jury pool. "I'm going to swear you in as a group so the attorneys and I can ask you some questions."

Tricia slipped into her prosecutorial duties as the routine of the trial began. It took two hours to seat the jury. Not long, considering. At one point Sydney slipped her a note that Linda had stepped out but Sydney would wait with her in the hallway since the defense had requested that all witnesses be sequestered.

Once she seated the jury and excused those who wouldn't be needed, Judge Sinclair turned to Tricia. "Ready for opening statements?"

Tricia nodded and stood. She approached the podium, her gaze locked on the jury. "Ladies and gentlemen, the case you will hear today centers on an incident of domestic violence. The crime of domestic assault occurs when a household member intentionally and knowingly causes bodily injury to his intimate partner. As the state will show today, that happened between Andrew and Linda Parker.

"Mr. Parker chose to attack his wife. In the course of the attack he broke her jaw and beat her. The couple's children were present for and watched the incident.

"The state will present evidence that Mrs. Parker was injured, her injuries were severe and consistent with abuse. You will hear from Linda, the police who responded to the 911 call, and her treating doctors." Tricia walked them through the evidence she'd present as well as the standard they were to apply as they evaluated the testimony and exhibits.

A buzz of adrenaline flowed through her. She practiced law for the chance to protect victims and seek justice. Hopefully, that's what she'd get a chance to do today. Her words flowed with fresh passion.

"Thank you in advance for your time and attention today. This process is truly what makes the United States a great nation." She turned to Judge Sinclair. "Thank you, your honor."

"Mr. Montgomery?"

"Thank you." Earl rose, dressed in his standard trial uniform of khakis and sports jacket, as if looking casual would sway a jury. "Members of the jury, you'll hear much today. Your challenge? Sift through the words until you uncover the truth. My client is a respected member of this community. You'll hear ample testimony that he is not a man who would do something like this, despite what the prosecutor will allege.

"You'll hear how Mrs. Parker has a history of injuring herself to get attention. Well, this time she did a number on herself."

Tricia bounced from her chair. "Objection, your honor. He's maligning a witness."

"Nothing that won't come out in testimony." He smiled at her with a smarmy smile that suggested he knew something she didn't. Earl usually behaved collegially, even if he was a tad eccentric. A coil of tension tightened in her gut, replacing the jazzed-up feeling she'd had minutes before. What did he have up his sleeve?

"Overruled, but tread carefully, Mr. Montgomery. Please proceed."

He rattled on with his opening statement, and Tricia fought to focus. A snake slid around her stomach, warning her that something was up. Something she wouldn't like.

She stole a glance at Andrew, caught him watching her. His eyes were cold and empty, with a flicker of something sharp. His mouth tipped in a shadow of the rakish grin that used to turn her into putty in his hands. Now it seared across her heart like a slap.

With effort she pulled away from his gaze. *God, help me.* She reached for the pitcher of water on the table, hand shaking. She had to get control of her emotions.

Finally, it was time to call her first witness. She walked through a routine examination of the responding officer. Cross-examination was minimal as Montgomery made the wise choice to get him off the stand quickly. Drawing a deep breath, Tricia called Linda to the stand.

Linda looked straight ahead as she pushed past the bar and stopped in front of the judge. After being sworn in, she settled into the witness chair, the seat creaking as she shifted against it. After the preliminaries like name and address were entered for the record, Tricia turned to the crux of the case.

"What happened the evening of May 16th?"

"Andrew came home from work agitated. He got worse as the evening progressed. First chance he got, he started hitting me."

"Had this happened before?"

"Not hitting me, but he's verbally abused me frequently when he gets angry."

Tricia walked her through what the verbal abuse had looked like. Then she turned back to the night in question. "Why did he start hitting you this time?"

"Because he wanted to." She looked straight ahead at the jury, unflinching as she spoke. "Andrew's had an anger problem for years. The words have been bad. They've been ugly. But he'd been drinking and this...this was the first time he hit me. I tried to endure it thinking he would realize what he was doing, but he didn't stop. I felt my jaw crack and started screaming for help."

"Did anyone witness the attack?"

"Our boys." Linda wiped under her eyes. "They watched their dad throw me to the floor and kick me. He broke my jaw and bruised my ribs. He didn't care that our children were huddled in the corner crying." She sniffed. "The boys are scared he'll do something to them."

"No further questions."

Earl stood and moseyed to the podium. "So Andrew came home 'angry.'"

Linda ignored him.

"Didn't you start picking at him the moment he walked in the door?"

"No."

"Really?" He raised his eyebrows and made a face at the jury. "Didn't you fall down the stairs? Inflict these wounds on yourself?"

Her nostrils flared, and she turned to him for the first time. "No. I did not injure myself." She turned back to the jury. "Have you ever suffered bruised ribs or a broken jaw? I doubt it, Mr. Montgomery, because if you had, you'd know that's a ridiculous question. No one in their right mind would do that to themselves."

"No further questions for this witness at this time, your honor."

Linda looked at Tricia, as if asking what to do next. Tricia nodded, as the judge told her she could step down and then broke for lunch. Through the break, Tricia huddled in her office. What else did Earl plan to say?

After lunch, Tricia interviewed Linda's treating physician at the emergency room, who talked the jury through the x-rays that showed her broken jaw and cracked ribs. Then Linda's primary care doctor talked about the on-going treatment and concerns. At the close of his testimony, Tricia took a moment to review her notes. There was nothing more that she could add that would help the journey. Either they understood this was an open and shut case of domestic battery or they didn't.

"Prosecution rests."

Earl stood and preened in front of the jury. "The defense calls Andrew Parker."

Andrew sauntered to the stand, as if the world would bow at his feet. So far it had. Tricia prayed the tide was turning. Each time she thought of his little boys cowering as he beat Linda, she felt sick. But today Linda had stood up to him, and the future could change. Tricia couldn't correct her past with the man, but she could finish this for Linda.

Tricia kept her eyes on Andrew as she scribbled notes on her legal pad as fast as Andrew talked. He gave his sorry account of the night. Blame it on the woman. Such an original argument. Linda hadn't egged Andrew on to violence. He didn't need any encouragement. She rubbed her scar, then looked up to see Andrew watching her as he talked. She pulled her hand down and fiddled with her pen.

"Anything else you want the judge and jury to know?" Earl asked in a way that sounded dangerous.

"One thing." He leaned forward in his seat until his lips practically brushed the microphone. "See that pretty attorney over there?" He gestured toward Tricia, and her heart sank to her toes.

The jury sat forward, and Tricia looked straight ahead, avoiding everyone's gaze. This could not be happening.

"She's not as squeaky clean as she'd like you to believe. We knew each other, quite well in fact..."

"Objection, your honor." Sydney jumped up from her seat behind the bar. "Relevance. This has nothing to do with the charges."

"Your honor, she can't object. She's not prosecuting this case."

"I am now. The defendant made my co-counsel a possible witness in this case."

Murmurs swept through the jury, the press pool, and the others in the courtroom. Judge Sinclair frowned and crossed her arms. "Ladies and gentlemen, we are in a courtroom—my courtroom—and I require decorum. Fifteen-minute recess." She stared at Tricia. "I recommend that you and your co-counsel discuss this before we reconvene."

Tricia stood as the judge and jury exited the room. Once they disappeared, she sank to her chair. What now? Reality had become worse than her nightmares.

"Wow, you've got yourself in a real mess, girlfriend." Sydney leaned closer. What's going on?"

Tricia groaned. "Why do you think I wanted out of this case?"

"Well, get ready to be called as a witness. Good thing I've listened to you moan about this case and sat in today. I think we've got the basics covered. Now you need to tell me, *Reader's Digest* version, what happened between you and Andrew?"

"The knight who turned into a beast. He raped and beat me when we were in college."

The blood drained from Sydney's face. "Oh, Tricia."

"Don't." She could be strong. Freedom had come when she revealed the past to Caleb, to Linda. She prayed the same would happen here if she released the last vestiges of shame. She had to accept that what had happened wasn't her fault. Her heart stuttered at the thought of sitting in the witness chair and sharing the darkest pieces of her past with the world. But she would do it if she had to.

She lifted her chin and stiffened her spine. Steeled herself for the ordeal ahead. It might be ten years later than it should have been. But the time had finally come to hold Andrew Parker accountable. For everything he'd done.

17

M*onday*

Noah slipped into the back of the courtroom. He'd spent the day chasing down his theory. The trail showed signs of life. Definitely worth pursuing. He couldn't wait to sit down with Tricia after this trial wrapped up and pick her brain. Between the two of them, they might figure out who set the fires before he set another one.

They had to, because Noah sensed that the time before the next fire would expire soon.

The uncertainty of where that strike would come had him edgy.

The courtroom buzzed with whispered conversations. Noah leaned forward and tapped the guy in front of him on the shoulder. "What's got everyone so excited?"

"Are you kidding?" The guy's eyes danced with enthusiasm. He set his thin notebook on the chair arm and turned to Noah. "This routine trial has just exploded. Not only is pretty boy Andrew Parker on trial, but the prosecuting attorney is now a witness. I'm not sure how that works, and I've covered the crime beat for years."

Dani Richards slid past a couple of people and settled next to Noah. "This isn't good."

"Why?" Noah braced himself for the answer.

"I have no idea what's going on, but Tricia looked white as a sheet when Sydney led her from the courtroom."

"What do we do?"

"Pray. I think she's going to need every prayer she can get."

Noah nodded, his mind racing with the implications. The only reason she'd get called as a witness was if Andrew said something about their past. What advantage could he gain from that? Other than getting her off the case and making her miserable? For an abuser, was that enough motivation?

He leaned forward, elbows on his knees as he prayed and waited. Tension coiled the muscles in his shoulders. Tricia had such a core of strength he couldn't imagine what had turned her into a shadow of herself, but as she came back into the courtroom he saw that Dani hadn't exaggerated. Tricia sank into her chair at the prosecutor's table, back straight, gaze locked ahead, looking pale and shaken but determined.

Noah wished he could reach her. Let her know he'd come and that he cared. The jury reentered the room, followed quickly by the judge. Flashes of the prior trial snapped through Noah's mind as he waited.

"You may resume, Mr. Montgomery."

Andrew Parker bobbed and weaved through a few questions. After his attorney finished, the attorney next to Tricia didn't have luck pinning him down. Then Montgomery stood. "Defense calls Tricia Jamison as a hostile witness."

A woman seated next to Tricia launched from her seat. "Objection, your honor. The defense did not list Miss Jamison on its witness list, and the prosecution hasn't prepared her. Even so, you can't allow them to treat her as a hostile witness."

"Counsel?" The judge looked over her glasses at the snake who preened for the jury.

"We didn't know we'd call her until now, but retained the right on our witness list to call any necessary witness. As you'll soon hear, she should have anticipated we might call her. And she's prosecuted the case to this point, making her hostile."

Tricia scribbled something on a notepad, and the other gal read it. "Your honor, a general reservation isn't enough to call the attorney for the other side as a witness. His failure to follow established rules of trial procedure can't be endorsed by this court."

The judge watched Tricia for a moment. Tricia's shoulders remained pushed back, and she looked straight ahead. Noah prayed...hard. Surely the judge would allow the objection, would protect Tricia from whatever the defense had planned.

Tapping a pen against her mouth, the judge waited while the silence stretched in the courtroom. One jury member shifted in his seat, while another looked at her watch. It couldn't be a good sign when the jury got restless.

Come on, judge.

She nodded as if making a decision. "I'm sorry, Tricia, but I'll allow your testimony, and I'll allow the defense to treat you as a hostile witness. Counsel, do you need a brief recess to prepare your witness?"

The woman looked at Tricia, who shook her head. "No, your honor."

"Miss Jamison."

Tricia rose to her feet. She moved to stand in front of the judge. As she raised her hand, all eyes in the room focused on her.

Tricia eased into the witness chair. The leather felt cold against her legs, and the microphone loomed in front of her. She perched on the edge and tried to still her heart as it beat hard against her chest.

She did not belong here. She felt like an Purdue cheerleader on the Cornhuskers sidelines—sorely out of place. But she had to do this.

God, help me. He'd promised to always walk with her. She clung to that promise as she opened her eyes and saw Noah and Dani seated against the back wall. Noah had bowed his head, but looked up and met her gaze. He gave her a subtle thumbs-up, followed by a finger pointed toward heaven. He mouthed something she couldn't read, but it didn't matter. He was here. God knew she'd need somebody supporting her and had surrounded her with friends and believers. Between Sydney, Dani, Noah and God, she could do this. Earl walked her through the preliminaries, and she tried to focus. Name, address, occupation. The easy questions finished, he paused, and she took a breath, steeling herself for what would come next.

"Miss Jamison, is it true you and the defendant had a relationship in the past?"

She licked lips suddenly dry as the Sahara. "Yes."

"Didn't you date in college?"

"Yes."

"And not just one or two dates. Didn't you date the defendant for over a year?"

Tricia nodded, heat rising up her neck.

"Please state your answer for the court reporter."

"Yes."

Earl glanced at his legal pad, as if checking his place. He returned his gaze to her face. "In fact, didn't you describe Andrew as your knight in shining armor?"

"Only in the early days of our relationship, before he showed his true colors." Tricia shifted against the seat, the leather sticking to the back of her legs.

"It's a yes or no question."

Tricia smiled. Had Earl really meant to emphasize her answer? "I suppose I did before I knew better. Yes."

Earl crossed his arms and stared down his nose at her. "You created this whole case because the defendant didn't continue your relationship, didn't you?"

"No." Tricia met the gaze of the jury. They had to believe her. She wouldn't do something like that. Ever. "Why would I? That was years ago?"

"You're an intelligent woman. You wouldn't go out with anyone, especially for that length of time, who mistreated you."

"But I did. He raped me..."

The entire courtroom fell silent...including Earl who looked at her with a dumbstruck expression.

What would he do?

Ask another question he didn't know the answer to?

Push her on why she didn't file a report with the police?

Did he know the right details?

She tried to breath and keep her composure even as she felt her body tremble from the stomach out, like she'd been out in bone chilling, wet day.

He turned to his client, who maintained an amazingly composed facade. Clearly Andrew hadn't shared all the details of their past. Relief flooded Tricia. Yes, Earl wasn't her favorite person, but at least he hadn't known the full story before putting her through this. Earl pulled himself together, and flipped a page on his legal pad, then looked at her. "No further questions." Earl threw the pad on the defense table then dropped into his chair. Tricia could imagine the conversation he'd have with his client when this was over.

"Counsel?" The judge looked at Sydney, with a look that showed she wondered what would happen next.

Sydney eased to her feet and looked at Tricia. "You just testified that the defendant raped you."

"Yes."

"When did this happen?"

"Almost a year into our relationship."

"What was your relationship prior to this point?"

Tricia closed her eyes, scenes playing through her mind. She opened her eyes and looked over the jury. "What started out so beautifully faded into nonstop manipulation. It started with jealousy. He constantly checked on me, wanted to know what I was doing, who I was with. Then his words became violent and abusive." One woman on the jury clearly didn't buy her testimony. "I don't know why I didn't leave him then. It's a question I've asked myself many times, but I believed I needed him. That without him my life would be empty. Then he became physically violent. I knew I had to leave, had to escape before he escalated again."

Earl launched from his chair. "Objection, your honor." The judge looked at Sydney, who responded, "Defense counsel opened this entire line of questioning when he put Ms. Jamison on the stand and asked about her relationship with the defendant. He can't suddenly change the rules."

The judge considered a moment, tapping her glasses against her chin. "You may proceed."

"Why didn't you file a police report or press charges?" Sydney continued.

"Because he threatened me. Told me what had happened was nothing compared to what he would do."

Sydney quirked an eyebrow at her. "You're a prosecutor. Why did you believe him?"

"I wasn't a prosecutor then." Tricia took a deep breath, tried to think of the best way to explain her frame of mind to the jury. She leaned forward. "Andrew swept into my world with romance and wonderful promises of what the future would be like. But they were promises he never intended to keep. And after he broke me down, he turned me into a punching bag and violated me. I felt powerless. That's exactly why I went to law school and became a prosecutor. I didn't want anyone else to feel the way I did then."

"Why prosecute this case?"

"Initially, I didn't want it." Tricia slowly shook her head as she remembered the heated exchange with her boss. "I tried to get it reassigned, but everyone's overworked. Then I realized this was an opportunity to stand up to him. I didn't years ago, but his wife wanted the violence to stop. This case is about what Mr. Parker is doing to his wife and family. It's about what's happening right now. The county attorney's office routinely prosecutes men who beat their wives and send them to the hospital." A rush of peace flowed through her as she sped up. "We uphold the law, Mr. Parker violated it. The county attorney assigned the case to me and I did my job."

"Is there anything else you would like the jury to know?"

Tricia turned to look at the jury. She took a moment to connect with each member. "I'm not proud of my past relationship with the defendant. I wish it had never happened. But it did. And I have lived with the things he did to me. Mrs. Parker's testimony makes it clear that he has not changed. Please do something to prevent him from continuing to do harm."

Sydney turned to the judge. "The prosecution has no further questions for this witness."

"Mr. Montgomery?"

"No questions, your honor."

"Then we'll recess for the night." She instructed the jury, then followed them out of the room.

Tricia stood and walked to the table. She could feel the weight of gazes on her, but kept her head high and her shoulders back. The peace continued to engulf her. How could bringing the past into the light bring such freedom? She gathered her things, hoping the room would clear while she did. Instead, the media started shouting her name.

Sydney gave her a quick hug. "You handled that well, Tricia. Let me go talk to Charlie, figure out what's next."

Tricia nodded, then sank into the chair. The bar squeaked as Earl and Andrew left. It squeaked again, but she didn't look up.

"Trish?" Noah crouched beside her chair. "You okay?"

"Yes. But how do I get past the media?" She kept her gaze focused on him, trying to ignore the frenzy behind him. She might feel lighter, but she didn't want to imagine what the newspaper headlines would look like in the morning. "Can you get me out of here?"

"No problem."

Dani grabbed the reporters' attention, got them to make a path as Noah hustled her through. She resisted the urge to hide behind him as cameras flashed a staccato accompaniment.

~

NOAH KEPT an eye on Tricia as she walked, tucked next to him as they moved through the reporters. He held his left arm out to create some space and hurried past, a move he was too familiar with thanks to the earlier trial. He felt the silence and needed to say something, but felt powerless. Fixing what had happened to her lay beyond his ability. Yet he was astonished at how calmly this strong, self-assured woman had handled an impossible situation.

She was an amazing woman. One with a core of strength she could use to pull her through whatever the next days held.

Noah ushered Tricia out a side entrance of the building, then stopped when there were no reporters waiting and blinked in the sunlight. "Where can I take you?"

"Home." Her voice sounded steady, but small, the word faint, as if the full weight of everything that had happened in the courtroom had settled on her. She shook her head. "On second thought, I'm not ready to go home."

"How about a small detour?"

She nodded, then followed him to his truck. He drove east on A Street, and then south on 70th until he hit the Holmes Lake area. The early evening was too nice to hide inside a building. Maybe a taste of creation could blow away any lingering memories brought back by her testimony.

"How do you do it?"

Tricia turned to look at him. "Do what?"

"You handled that testimony with a grace I know I wouldn't have had."

"I don't know." She shrugged. "I guess God is making sure I deal with all the baggage from my past. Maybe it's time to move into the future."

Noah parked the truck, then hopped out and opened her door. "Do you want to walk around the lake?"

Tricia accepted his help as she climbed from the truck. "All right. Though I don't know how fast I can go in these shoes." He looked down at the spiky heels she called shoes. "Maybe we should sit on a bench instead. If the day were nicer, I'd go across the street to my apartment. Grab my canoe, and get you in the middle of the lake. There's nothing like it." The wind whipped up miniature whitecaps. Not the best day for canoeing, even if he felt he could do it without straining his knee.

A smile crossed Tricia's face. "I'm okay, Noah."

He studied her face carefully. "You know, I think you are. God answered our prayers."

"If only He could have made the press deaf and dumb for the time I testified." A soft sigh filtered to his ear. "I can't imagine what tomorrow will be like."

Geese honked in the distance as they took turns lifting from the water's surface and returning to it. His pager vibrated against his hip. Noah looked at the number then grabbed his cell phone and dialed.

"Brust. You paged?"

Tricia looked at him, questions in her eyes. He held up a finger and shook his head as he tried to listen to the dispatcher. Another fire blazed, and Weary wanted him on-site.

"All right. What's the address?" Noah repeated the address, then heard a gasp next to him as Tricia grabbed his arm. His gut tightened as the location registered. That was her address. He hung up and turned to Tricia. "I'll get you there fast."

Tricia's chin quivered and she dropped his arm and kicked off her shoes. After scooping them up, she raced to his truck, and Noah followed on her heels, unlocking her door. Once she was seated, he ran to the driver's side and climbed in.

As his beeper sounded again, Noah prepared for the worst.

18

M*onday*

Traffic stalled as Noah tried to turn left out of Holmes Lake Park onto 70th. Tricia pushed her feet into the floor of the truck, wishing she could force a hole in the traffic to appear. Didn't people understand?

Something had happened at her house. Flames licking her roof filled her imagination.

Heat scorched her at the thought. She bit the inside of her lip. The pain had to keep the tears from falling. She reminded herself to trust God. Somehow, no matter what she found at the house, she would get through it. If God had given her the strength to get through the testimony this afternoon—something that had seemed impossible—He could do the same again. He'd promised He wouldn't give her more than she could handle. As they neared her house, she wondered how much more He expected her to endure.

The house served as her ark, her place of refuge from the storms of life. She always felt safe there. Protected. Secure. Not anymore.

A metallic taste filled her mouth as she bit the inside of her cheek, but it didn't stop the tears that streamed down her cheeks.

"Can't you go faster?" She knew he couldn't. Could see it with her eyes. But...

"I'll get you there as quickly as I can. In one piece." He turned back and forth, hunting for a break in the cars, but the rush-hour traffic stalled. "Lord, we could use some help."

Finally, a break in the stream of cars. Noah barreled his truck into the opening.

Tricia needed to pray. She had to grab hold of God, ask for His protection. But fear filled her. What if the fire blazed out of control? What if she lost everything? Where would she stay? What would she do? The questions raced around her mind. "Did they say anything about the fire? How bad is it?" She looked at Noah, begging him for details.

"I don't know. Dispatch didn't say anything more than it's a fire."

"Who would do this?"

He glanced over at her, then looked out the windshield. "We'll find out. I promise."

~

NOAH WATCHED her from the corner of his eye. Tricia had a brittle edge that made her look as if she'd shatter if one more thing went against her. He suspected arson, but had to keep an open mind or he couldn't participate in the investigation. He needed to be part of the team that brought an end to the destruction and found justice for Tricia.

He pulled the truck in and out of traffic. If he were traveling alone, he'd call the dispatcher and get an update, but he didn't want to risk bad news. Better to see whatever Tricia would face without the challenge of information passed along secondhand.

Finally, traffic eased as he turned on Vine and headed west. As they neared 40th, a billow of thick smoke spiraled into the sky. The familiar aroma seeped into the truck. Based on the column, it appeared that more than a shed was burning. "Do you have a detached garage?"

"No. Just parking in the driveway. Is it bad?"

Noah frowned and stared at the heavy gray smoke. "We'll know in a minute. Where was Jessie?"

Tricia's face blanched. "I'd let her out, but I tied her near the door so she wouldn't slip under the fence."

Another reason to get to her house now. He whipped onto a side street, then followed the flashing lights. Fire trucks blocked the street, but he created a spot next to a pumper truck.

Tricia gasped, and he turned to find her thin control evaporated. Tears coursed down her cheeks as she watched the yellow and red flames consume her home. The windows on the front had exploded outward. If Jessie had been tied close to the door... Noah didn't want to finish that thought.

A police car pulled up, and two officers hopped out and worked to establish a perimeter. People stood around the perimeter and shuffled back at the urging of the officers. Noah scanned the crowd. At first glance, none of the faces looked familiar. "Tricia, reach under the seat. You should find a camera. I need it now."

She looked at him a moment, then leaned over and felt along the floorboards. "Is this what you want?" She tugged a bag from the side.

"Yep." He took the bag and unzipped it. She jumped out of the truck while he hit the on button and waited for the camera to comply. "Come on." Finally, the screen turned on, and Noah pointed the camera out the window and began shooting photos.

"What are you doing?"

"Shooting the bystanders. Sometimes we can ID someone after the fact who's been at several fires. Or if we see someone walking away from the fire, rather than toward the fire, it's another sign they could be involved." He shot a couple more, then scrolled through the photos. They weren't close, but hopefully he'd get a clear enlargement.

Tricia watched the activity around her house. The flames reflected off her face. From what he could see, she wouldn't have much to salvage.

She shuddered, and he reached over to wipe tears from her

cheeks. Tricia leaned into his touch. "Why? Why would someone do this to me?"

"We'll find out. I promise." He hated to leave her, but wanted to get a closer look at the fire, maybe search for some sign that Jessie had gotten away. "I'll be back in a minute."

Noah bypassed the perimeter established by the police and pulled out his cell phone. He dialed Caleb's number and waited for him to pick up. Instead, he heard the annoying voice telling him he could leave a message. Definitely not what he wanted to do, not when Tricia needed Caleb.

A Channel 13 truck pulled up, and other media would follow soon. Dani Richards hopped out of the passenger side. "Where is she?"

"By my truck."

"All right." She spun on her heel and hightailed it to the vehicle.

Noah released his breath. Dani would stay with Tricia. Now he could focus where he should. On the fire. A frantic bark sounded from the backyard, matched by the rattle of the chain-link fence. Noah hurried around the perimeter to the fence. Jessie cowered in the corner nearest the alley.

"Come here, girl."

She looked at him and whined, but didn't move. Noah hurried around the fence to the alley. He unlatched the gate, expecting Jessie to bolt and get as far away from the flames as possible. Instead, she jerked around in a stilted dance. "What's wrong, Jess?"

Stepping into the yard, Noah approached her slowly. She whined and wiggled. When he reached her, he ran his hand along her collar and found a rope. Someone had tied her to the fence. Who would have moved her from where Tricia had left her? He slipped her from the fence, keeping the rope attached as a leash to get her through the chaos and back to the truck.

Dani saw him and nodded before heading back to the news vehicle.

He hurried to Tricia, but she didn't see him, her gaze focused on the flames. "Tricia, take Jessie."

"What?" Tricia startled when she saw the dog. "Jessie." She knelt and held out a hand to the dog. "Girl, I was worried about you."

Noah watched the two interact for a minute. "Tricia, can you put her in the cab and sit with her a bit? She's more than a little stressed."

"Okay."

Noah stowed Jessie in the cab, and then returned to the scene.

Firefighters trained several hoses on the house. The rush of water contained the fire, but its fury hadn't lessened.

Noah turned back to check on Tricia. She was sitting in the truck with Jessie's head on her shoulder, stroking the dog's fur. A shuttered look covered her face. She stared ahead, as if mesmerized by the flames. Dani had returned to the truck and leaned against the door, talking to her through the open window. Tricia didn't respond.

She shouldn't watch this. Nothing good could come from watching her home disintegrate into ash. Noah rubbed the back of his neck.

She needed someone.

No, she needed him.

She might not admit it, but the fact remained. No one should endure alone what she had today. And he wanted to be the one who'd be there for her.

He looked at the blaze. The responding unit had it under control. He couldn't do anything else until the flames had died down and he could examine the exterior of the house. Until then, he would focus on Tricia.

He stepped away from the heat of the flames to the passenger side of his truck. "Dani."

"Hi, Noah." The light that usually shone from her eyes had dimmed. "Any thoughts on the fire?"

"As a friend or reporter?"

A sad smile tipped her face. "A friend."

"It's too early. I'll have to wait until I can check the perimeter. Rule out all other causes first." Tricia had turned and listened to their conversation. "Are you up for a few questions?"

She shook her head, then nodded. "I thought I'd answered enough today."

The flash of spunk pleased him. She'd bounce back. Under it all, she had the heart of a fighter. "Have you had any contractors at your house lately? Any work done on the furnace? Water heater? Electrical system?"

Tricia frowned. "No. I haven't had any problems with the house. Nothing that required contractors."

"Anyone loitering around?"

"No."

"Notice anyone watching you? A car that doesn't belong to a neighbor on the street?"

"No. I haven't noticed anything. I would have over the weekend. Besides you and Caleb were here Saturday night. And Jessie didn't seem to notice anything."

Noah shoved his hands deep in his jean pockets. "Where will you stay tonight?"

Tricia seemed to shrink inside her suit jacket. "I don't know."

"With me, of course." Dani looked exasperated that Tricia hadn't known. "You did the same for me."

"Nobody's stalking me."

"No. All the more reason you should stay with me. I won't be in danger." Dani grinned. "We'll have to do a bit of shopping, too."

Tricia groaned. "That's the last thing I want to do tonight." She stared at the fire, then seemed to pull strength from somewhere inside herself. "I'll be doing lots of things I don't want to in the next few weeks." She turned to Noah, locking on his gaze. "We have to find whoever did this. Before they harm anybody else."

"We will." He promised himself. Nothing else mattered until they figured out why someone was starting these fires. "I've been working on this case over the weekend. I think I'm closer to a motivation from that 'a-ha' thought I had on Saturday. The key question— What connects you and me?"

19

M*onday*

What connected her and Noah? The question was the next right one to answer, since Caleb's efforts to hunt through his files for answers and suspects hadn't identified any reasonable suspects. The other fires dimmed when compared to the severity of the one consuming her home.

Tricia could feel the flames' heat from Noah's truck as she watched the flames lick her home.

The other fires served as warm-up acts.

They set the stage. Did this one punctuate the arsonist's statement or would he set even more fires?

This wasn't the end. Fingers of fear crawled up her spine at the thought. They had to find him...now.

This guy was on a fast path of acceleration.

Noah looked down as his phone sang a muffled song, then answered. "Brust."

He turned away from her and Dani. "Sir, the fire's fully engulfed the house. There won't be much to salvage." He listened for a moment, then walked away with an apologetic look over his shoulder. He seemed to communicate a promise with that look. Here at last was the man who wanted to be her knight in shining armor. She felt the attraction, and wanted to explore what the future might hold.

As the flames consumed the remnants of her home, she wondered if Noah would provide a level of stability to a life that was being stripped bare one flame at a time. The enormity of everything fell on her. All the things she had thought defined her life were burning up in front of her eyes. She didn't have a home. Her job could never be quite the same after everything that had happened earlier in court. She'd have a lot of explaining to do in the morning about why she hadn't told anyone about her history with Andrew Parker. But in spite of it all, she felt surprisingly calm. She'd lose the "things" in her life, but she found herself closer to the people who mattered to her. Maybe her possessions were like her past—something else God wanted her to release.

Noah stamped his feet as he hung up the phone. A thin mist of water hung in the air. The truck protected her, but not the others, from the dampness. In the cold, the dampness went from miserable to dangerous.

Tricia turned to Dani. "You need to get back to the TV station Jeep. Caleb will have a fit."

"No, he'll be angry he wasn't here when you needed him."

He couldn't do anything other than watch the destruction with her. She'd need him more later on.

Dani reached in her pocket and pulled out her keys. "Tricia, here's my house key. I won't get home until after the six o'clock newscast, but this way you don't have to wait."

Collapsing in Dani's guestroom sounded wonderful.

Noah walked from the house back to his truck.

"You'll get her to my house, right?" Dani gestured across the street. "I'm not far in that direction. Vine and 33rd area."

"I'll find it."

"Okay. Job and Jessie should get along fine." She leaned in and hugged Tricia. "I'll see you as soon as Logan and I get these packages put together."

Noah walked around the truck. "I'll stay with her until you get back."

Tricia frowned at his tone. "I don't think I'm in danger. The guy behind this hasn't killed anyone. In fact, I'd say he's been very careful."

"So far." The tone in Noah's voice sent shivers skittering up and down her spine.

Dani shook her head. "I did not need that image. See you in a bit."

A strange comfort crept under the haze filling Tricia as she held onto Jessie. She might have lost her home, but so far she had no reason to fear for her life. All the more reason to find the person behind this before he escalated to an entirely new crime.

"Do you need anything before we head to Dani's?"

She'd need a lot before she could go anywhere in the morning. "Probably."

"Target it is. Then you can direct me to Dani's." He got behind the wheel and started on a detour east to 48th Street.

She tried to ignore his presence as she ran through the aisles collecting the essentials: makeup, clothes, deodorant. By the time they returned to his truck, the adrenaline had subsided.

"Have you eaten today?" Noah eyed her, concern on his face.

"Is it that obvious?" Tricia leaned her head against the side window, feeling the chill soak into her skin. "I don't feel like eating, but I should."

"What sounds good?"

Her stomach flipped at the thought. She put her hand over her mouth and swallowed. "Maybe a shake."

Noah nodded. He pulled into a drive-through and a few minutes later handed her a vanilla shake. She sipped as he drove the few blocks to Dani's home.

"You'll have to park in back since there isn't any street parking."

"Is that safe?"

Tricia laughed. "I don't think you have to worry about her neighborhood. Job's the issue."

Questions filled Noah's eyes as he glanced at her.

"Her dog. Job's a big mongrel with a great attitude once he knows you. Before that, watch out. He sounds fierce."

Noah pulled into the alley, then waited while Tricia led the way. "Let's introduce Jessie from this side of the fence."

Noah watched Tricia talk Job down. Job had turned to putty as she whispered and petted him. But she didn't seem to be making any progress in bringing Job to them. If she kept it up, they'd stand outside all night. "Trish."

She looked up. "Oh. Sorry. Come on, Jessie." She slipped inside the fence and pulled Jessie with her. In an instant, Jessie was on her back, paws in the air, the picture of submission. He almost laughed at the image.

Tricia smiled and led the way up the sidewalk to the back door. A motion-activated light kicked on, illuminating the stoop. Tricia opened the door and stepped into a kitchen. "Here we are."

He eased onto a barstool. "Have you called Caleb yet?"

"Dani and I each left him a message. He'll come tearing up the street as soon as he can." She rubbed at the pounding in her temples. "He's going to hate that he didn't catch the arsonist before he destroyed my house. So much has happened in the last few days. Now this."

"While we wait for him to get the word and arrive, I want to run my theory by you."

"Okay." She grabbed a couple of glasses from a cupboard and filled them with water. "What do you have?"

"Your family's been hit, and if you're right, I was targeted by the arsonist, too. Each fire in your family has been more destructive than the previous ones. At this point, I think we're the arsonist's targets."

She stared through him, and he could almost see the thought churning around her mind. "But why? I still don't see any motivation, and this seems pretty personal."

"How did we meet?"

"The Lincoln Life trial."

"What if whoever's involved is upset about that trial?"

"Maybe." Tricia chewed on a fingernail. "I agree that's what's linked us in the past. But why act now? And why not go after the prosecutor who led the case or another witness? Why us?"

Noah leaned his elbows on the island and steepled his fingers. "I don't know. But until we have a better idea, work with me on this one."

"So who are the suspects?" she asked.

"The families who lost someone in the fire?"

Tricia nodded. "That's a start. Including firefighters, fifteen people died."

"Which were the most painful losses?" She looked at him with confusion. "I mean spouse killed, child, things like that."

"That covers all the families." Tricia rubbed her forehead then turned toward the hallway. "Let me get some paper from Dani's office. We can chart this out."

Her heels clacked against the hardwood floors and up the stairs. A minute later, she returned to the kitchen, two pads of paper and pens in hand.

Six firefighters and nine civilians died in the fire. Tricia drew a grid and inserted names and occupations. Noah studied the names. "Do you know any of the civilians? I can fill in background info on most of the firemen. Bobby was single and a loner. I don't think he had anyone who would avenge his death like this."

Tricia studied his name as if envisioning his file. "I don't remember anyone suing on his behalf. And he didn't have a beneficiary listed on his life insurance policy, so you're probably right." She drew a check mark in the corner of Bobby's square. She looked at the other names and doodled squiggles and lines across the bottom. "I didn't work the entire case. We need access to the files."

"Can you get them?" he asked.

"Should be able to, but if they're in cold storage, it'll take a day or two." Tricia paced along the counters. "There have to be other angles we haven't thought about. Who's called these fires in?"

Noah frowned, trying to figure out what direction she was headed. "I don't know."

"Wouldn't dispatch or whoever takes the 911 call have that information?"

"Yes, there would be a tape of the call."

"Wouldn't they have location information? Where the call originated?"

"It depends."

"That's a legal answer."

"Not this time. If the call was made from a landline, then, yes, that information should have been captured by the dispatcher. But if they called with a VOIP—" Tricia looked at him as if he spoke a different language "—Voice Over Internet Protocol—think Vonage—then the information might not be available."

"What about cell phones?"

"Same thing. Reasoning's different, but the results are the same. Unless the phone has a GPS card installed, the best you can hope for is a triangulation that still leaves ground to cover. Even with GPS, there aren't guarantees we'll get a lock." Noah watched her pace, then patted the stool next to him. "Sit down. You'll wear a path in the floor and you're making me nervous." Tricia grimaced. "I wish some part of this was easy."

"We're closing in."

"On a theory."

"Yes, but it's a theory we didn't have before."

The ghost of a smile teased Tricia's lips. "True." She eased next to him and sat down.

They both jumped when his phone rang, belting out the lyrics to a country song about leaving. "Brust."

Weary screamed in his ear. "Where are you?"

"Working on theories for the fires involving the Jamisons."

"That's what I thought. Stop."

"What?" Noah didn't try to hide the shock from his voice. "You're pulled from the case."

Noah turned away from Tricia, aware that she'd still hear every word. "You can't do that."

"Just did. You've been compromised."

20

M*onday*

The words hit her in the gut, leaving her empty. Noah removed from the investigation? Who would champion her cause? She stood, grabbed her bags and left the kitchen.

She had to get away from the conversation.

"Tricia, wait."

She shook her head and kept walking. She climbed the stairs and closed the guestroom door behind her.

Her phone vibrated inside her pocket. Tricia dug it out and studied the caller ID. Mom. Did she have the energy to talk to her? It didn't matter. Her mother would need to hear her voice, hear that she was okay. Tricia opened the phone and settled on the bed. "Hello."

"Baby, are you okay? Where are you? I'll come get you, bring you home." Mom's words raced over Tricia.

"I'm okay."

"Why didn't you call? I had to hear about the fire from Caleb. I'm worried sick about you."

Tricia rubbed her temple. "I was distracted by everything, but I'm sorry I worried you. All I could do was watch the flames. Then Noah brought me here."

"Where's here?"

"Dani's."

Silence. It stretched between them, pulling taut. "I don't understand why you wouldn't come here."

Tricia pinched the bridge of her nose. She didn't have the emotional reserves to go there right now. "Mom, I love you, but it made sense to come here." Feel safe.

A soft sigh. "How long will you stay with Dani?"

"Tonight." Tricia cleared her throat. "I'll call you tomorrow when I have a better idea what's next."

"Okay. Are you sure I can't come get you?"

"No. I'll call in the morning. Promise."

"All right. I love you, Tricia. Stay safe."

"Love you, too." Tricia closed the phone and pressed her forehead against it. She'd forgotten to tell Mom about the trial. What now?

Today had been too much. She pulled her knees to her chest. It felt like the nights she'd waited in bed, hyperalert for the sound of Frank padding down the hallway to her room. Only this time it wasn't a known enemy who hunted her, but an unknown.

God, are You still there?

She could give up her house, or even her job, but she needed to feel safe.

Instead, she felt so alone, especially now that Noah had been removed from the case. She longed for her Heavenly Father to hold her close.

She thought about her drive to work that morning. She'd listened to the radio, and the music had rolled over her. Harmonic voices belted out "I Need You to Love Me," a song that resonated to her core. As she thought of them now, the words soaked into her spirit. That's what she needed. To stop pretending and accept His love. The absolute assurance that God loved her, regardless of her past. That He had walked through it with her. She had to know He'd been there each moment, each day. And that His heart had broken with hers at each violation of trust and love.

That it still broke with her today.

Tricia sat another moment, eyes closed, and peace settled over her as she envisioned sitting under the shelter of His wing even in the middle of the storm.

A dull ache tugged Tricia from her dreamless sleep. She felt chilled, but someone had thrown a blanket over her. Tricia stretched with caution. Every muscle felt stiff, and her back rebelled at the treatment it had received. She cracked open her eyelids then slowly pushed up to a sitting position.

Voices filtered through the closed door. She turned on the bedside lamp and glanced at her watch. Three in the morning? Who did Dani have over at this hour?

Tricia eased to her feet, and then padded down the hall, pausing on the stairs when one creaked under her weight.

"Guess Sleeping Beauty decided to join us." Caleb's voice carried the tired tone of a big brother on overload.

Tricia hurried down the stairs and entered the room. She paused, sleep still fogging the corners of her mind. Caleb stood and gave her a hug. "I'm sorry about your house, Trish. I wish I could have done something to stop it."

In his words she heard an apology for so many things. She swallowed hard and leaned into his embrace. The comfort soaked through her.

He squeezed her and let go. "We'll get you through this."

Tricia looked up and saw the promise in his eyes.

Noah cleared his throat, and the world spun into motion again. He grinned at her. "How do I get a hug like that?"

Tricia stuck her tongue out at him, then looked for a place to sit. Why would he even want to be near her, looking like she must after the day she'd had? Exhaustion composed of more than fatigue weighed on her. Dani must have seen it, because she pushed out of her chair and grabbed another mug. "Need some coffee?"

"Absolutely." Tricia tousled her fingers through her hair. "Looks like I'll be up awhile."

"I tried to chase the guys out of here before they woke you. They seem determined to stay."

Noah stretched and yawned. "Call us stubborn. Besides, we're making progress."

"On what?" Tricia accepted the cup of coffee from Dani and walked over to the island. The chart she'd started hours earlier had bloomed across the page. Additional pages with scribbled notes surrounded its edges.

"Looking for relationships and suspects."

Caleb tapped one box. "I think Noah's onto something. The Lincoln Life fire may be the connection. But I think we should broaden our investigation to include the injured. Do you have numbers?"

Tricia rubbed her temples, trying to get her brain to wake up. "I dealt with a small piece of the overall case." She looked at Noah. "Fifteen killed, including the firemen, and twice that number injured."

"That sounds right."

"Any of the injured die later?" Caleb straddled a chair, propping his arms along the back.

"Maybe." She shrugged. "I can check on that and the names in a few hours when the office opens." Tricia picked up a pen and added to the doodles across the bottom. "You were taken off the case, Noah. Why are you still here?"

"You need me." He sighed, then slouched against the wall. "Weary isn't running with this theory. The only way to chase it is to work with you."

His words reached her. Maybe he would stick around, see this through to its resolution. Tricia felt a lump swell up her throat. She would not break down. Not this time. Noah had already seen far more weakness in her than any man should.

"Why don't you gals go to bed?" Caleb shoved his hands in his pockets. "Noah and I will keep working on the connections." Dani put her hands on her hips and stared at Caleb. "Why don't you admit you're watching over us?" She leaned over and pecked him on the cheek. "I think it's sweet." Was that red climbing Caleb's cheeks? "Come on, Tricia. Let's grab some pillows and blankets for these guys. None of us will get anything accomplished if we don't get a few hours' sleep." Tricia followed her to the basement, letting the cooler air wake her. "Did Noah mention why Weary removed him from the investigation?"

"No, but I don't think it came up." Dani pulled a couple of pillows off a shelf and threw them at Tricia. Tricia juggled them while Dani grabbed blankets. "He looked pretty subdued when I got here and wouldn't leave until Caleb arrived. One thing led to another, and it's after three." She let out such a big yawn that her jaw popped. "Ouch. I think you're on the right track. I'll see what I can learn about the victims when I get to the TV station in the morning."

Tricia followed Dani to the stairs. "Before we go up, do you think anything's salvageable at my house?"

Dani shook her head. "I'm sorry, Tricia, but we'll be doing a lot of shopping."

SILENCE STRETCHED while the men waited for Dani and Tricia to be out of earshot. Noah remained silent. Caleb would have to ask the question, because he wouldn't volunteer the information. Instead, Noah stared at his mug. It was the kind of cup his grandma would have. Silly cartoon drawing with a friendship message. Caleb had his work cut out for him, clearing the house of things like that after he married Dani.

"You were taken off the case." Caleb stated it, rather than asked.

"Weary says I'm compromised because everyone saw me comforting Tricia. He says I'm too emotionally involved."

Caleb studied him. "Are you?"

"Emotionally involved?"

"Yes."

"I am."

For a moment, there was silence then Caleb spoke. "Okay. We've got bigger issues to worry about."

Noah nodded. They certainly did.

Caleb continued. "We need to work together to get whoever is starting these fires. Frankly, I need help protecting Tricia and Dani. The most the department can do right now is send officers by on periodic patrols."

"I can stay tonight, help you here."

Caleb nodded, a rogue look in his eyes. "Good. I'll take the opportunity to determine if you're good enough for Tricia."

A soft gasp came from the doorway. Tricia stood there, mouth open, color in her cheeks. "Caleb."

"I'm your brother. I can investigate the guys who want to be part of your life." He turned toward Noah. "Wish I'd done that earlier."

Noah nodded. They all did.

Tricia crossed her arms. "Just make you sure you don't chase away the first man I've cared about in a long time."

He stilled at her words. Did she really mean that? She looked resolute, almost afraid, but intent to stand her ground.

Dani laughed. "Okay, you two. It's too late for this bantering. Tricia, you and I are going upstairs now. Gents, you lock the door on your way out, sleep on the couch, whatever. We're going to bed."

Dani tugged Tricia after her with a stop to dump the pillows and blankets they'd carried.

Noah kept an eye on Caleb, not sure what to do next.

Dani returned and approached Caleb, then took his face in her hands. "Tricia's right, Caleb. Don't get in the way while they see what's here."

Noah grinned at Dani. He'd take all the help he could get. She winked at him, then kissed Caleb and his shoulders slumped.

"You can't make up for the past by being overly protective now." Dani's soft voice settled around them.

"But I had fears about Frank." Caleb slumped against Dani. "I didn't do anything. I was too wrapped up in me, football, the next thing."

"She understands. But you have to treat her like the woman she is. She's scarred, but a big part of moving on is dealing with the past, not re-creating it."

Noah felt like an intruder watching them. There was such closeness in the way they talked and understood each other. That's what he wanted. With Tricia. But first he had to show her that he was dependable. That he would always be there. Always protect her. Noah moved to the kitchen to give Dani and Caleb some privacy.

Jessie whined at the back door, Job standing beside her. Noah opened the door and watched the dogs trot around the perimeter of the yard. He squinted into the darkness beyond the porch light. It looked like Jessie's hackles were standing on edge. Hmmm, hadn't taken her long to establish this as her area. He stepped onto the porch, ready to intervene if she decided to bark. Instead, a low growl reached his ears. He moved down a step. What did she see? Job stood at Jessie's side, nose pointed toward the alley.

A sensation crept up his back. Somebody was watching in the darkness. Noah leaned in the house. "Caleb, come here."

Noah didn't wait to see if Caleb responded. He hurried off the steps and into the yard. "Come here, girl."

Jessie looked at him, whined, then whipped her head back toward the fence. Something definitely bothered her. Too bad he couldn't see what it was.

"What do you need, Noah?" Caleb's voice carried too well in the early-morning stillness.

"I don't know, but something has the dogs on edge."

Caleb reached Noah's side and studied the animals. "I see what you mean." He snapped his fingers. "Job, come here." The dog didn't budge.

Noah stared into the alley, searching the shadows. "Thoughts?"

"Want to explore?"

"You're the policeman."

"Investigator."

"Yeah, so investigate."

Jessie whined and pawed at the gate. Job stood at attention and barked at the darkness. A strong odor tickled Noah's nose as the breeze carried it past them. Caleb crossed his arms and looked at Noah. "Is that what I think it is?"

"If you're thinking gasoline, yes." Noah looked down the alley to the left. "I think it's coming from this direction." Noah hopped over the fence without another glance. He didn't care if Caleb followed. All that mattered was locating the gasoline before another fire erupted.

His footsteps crunched in the gravel louder than he liked. No way he could sneak up on anyone who hid on the block. He heard a thump behind him. Caleb must have joined him after all.

A shadowy form hobbled from the shadows surrounding a garage at the end of the alley and hurried around the corner.

"Caleb, this way." Noah took off after him. His steps pounded, and he gained on the form. Then his foot slipped into a dip, and his knee popped. Pain shot from the joint up and down his leg. He collapsed on the ground and gritted his teeth. Caleb slowed when he saw him.

"Go after him. I'll still be here."

Without a word, Caleb tore down the rest of the alley, showing the speed he'd displayed on the football field in college. Noah twisted to inspect the alley. The scent of gasoline seemed stronger. Was that the flicker of a flame? Noah limped to his feet and pulled out his cell phone. Dialing 911, he called in the fire while he shuffle-stepped to the side of the garage. He looked around the alley in the dim light, looking for something that could subdue the flame before it reached the pool of gasoline.

Tires squealed. Homs blared a moment later. Caleb? Noah prayed Caleb was okay and had seen something. Even if his knee would let him, he couldn't run after Caleb until he'd extinguished the fire. Without foam, he needed sand, something to smother the flame and then cover the gasoline. Noah kicked dirt from the alley onto the flame. He clenched his teeth against the pain. He'd deal with it later. Groaning, he watched the flame crawl along the ground, seeming to pick up speed. Another kick or two. He had to keep it from reaching the garage. He might not have stopped the other fires, but he had a chance here. One last kick, and then he buckled. Looked for the flames. Extinguished. Finally.

Pain warred with anger.

He rolled to his side and pushed to his feet. Slowly he hobbled back to the fence.

How could he protect Tricia now?

21

Tuesday

The early morning darkness softened as Westmont drove his car away from the emergency room. Noah yawned and tried to connect with the big man. A couple of hours earlier he'd appreciated it when Caleb had called his police buddy to take Noah to the hospital rather than wake Tricia and Dani. Now, he just wanted to see the girls. Know Tricia was safe and secure.

Westmont refused to talk in more than grunts and one-word answers.

"Need to stop for coffee and donuts?"

Westmont looked at him with a frown. "Why?"

"Seems like you need your caffeine or sugar fix."

"Sorry. I hadn't gotten to bed when Caleb called."

"Oh."

"Yeah, I'd just wrapped up a double homicide."

"Thanks for driving me around when you could have slept."

"Consider me your personal bodyguard."

Noah looked at him, trying to find some trace that he'd meant the words as a joke. Unless he'd become a terrible people reader,

Westmont was dead serious. Noah shook his head. Nah, surely the pain meds had stuffed his head with cotton.

"So where you taking me now?"

"Home."

"I need to get back to Dani's. Someone has to keep an eye on the girls."

"Caleb's already got an officer assigned." Westmont turned down another road. "As long as either of the ladies is at the house, an armed officer will be there."

Noah rubbed his knee. "I still can't go home. Take me to the fire station. Somewhere. I need to find whoever was there last night. Got to get this thing solved before someone gets hurt."

Westmont tore his gaze from the road, looked at Noah and snorted.

"Okay, I get your point." Even though the knee was tightly wrapped and the doctor said he'd only sprained it, Noah didn't quite believe him. The lingering fear that he'd reinjured it in a way that would debilitate him gnawed.

"Following doctor's orders for you."

"Take me to Dani's then. I need my truck." The minute Westmont dropped him off, he'd climb in his truck and find Tricia.

As the car rolled along the road, Noah's thoughts reviewed everything that had happened in the last week. The scanner in the car buzzed to life periodically with calls of various sorts. Noah ignored the static.

Westmont's phone rang. Noah opened his eyes long enough to watch Westmont take the call.

"Yep." The man grunted. "On my way." He closed the phone. "Looks like we're making a detour."

~

TRICIA OPENED her eyes and tried to take in her surroundings. Sunlight streamed through a high window into a sunny yellow room that was not hers. She wrestled with the quilt she'd twisted around her body in the night. Slowly, everything came into focus. The fire. The need to stay with Dani. The fear that Noah would abandon her.

A million thoughts rushed through her mind at once. What should she do first? Go to work to finish the trial? Contact her insurance agent?

She hated the out-of-control feeling. Tricia wanted to tackle life first before it delivered a knockout punch. This time she couldn't. Instead, she'd have to depend on others.

A sharp knock rattled the door.

"Come in."

Dani breezed in, dressed in a tailored pantsuit paired with a green shirt that matched her emerald eyes. "Good morning, sleepyhead. I've got to get to the TV station. Sydney called on your cell. She's taking over the Parker trial, so you don't need to go in today. Charlie wants you to take the time you need to get your life back in order."

A pounding started behind her eyes, and Tricia rubbed her temples. She'd call Sydney later after she built the longest to-do list of her life. If only she knew where to start. Insurance. She'd need those funds to start rebuilding.

"Tylenol is in the medicine cabinet. Help yourself. Do you want me to take you to your car on my way to work?"

The thought of being trapped in the house was terrible. "I can be ready in thirty minutes."

"Make it twenty, and I'll take you."

Tricia flew through the shower, got dressed in some of her new clothes and applied minimal makeup. Her mind jumbled with things to do. She didn't know what steps to take to start pulling everything together. She'd need to get a notebook and start that list. She rushed down the steps and into the kitchen. Dani waited at the island, an extra cup of what smelled like coffee sitting in front of her.

"I've called the news director and let her know I'd be a bit late. Kate was surprisingly understanding." Dani patted the stool next to her. "Have a seat. I want to pray with you before we go." Tears filled Tricia's eyes. A year ago, Dani wouldn't have offered to pray. Now as

Tricia listened to her words, the prayer flowed naturally. The beauty of the words filled the empty places in Tricia's heart.

"Father, walk with Tricia today. Give her wisdom and prepare the path for her. We don't understand why You allowed the fire, but You did. So I ask You to do what You do best and turn what the enemy intended for evil into something good." Dani's words trailed to a stop.

Peace filled the room. Tricia basked in it a moment, letting it seep deep into her spirit. "Father, thank You. Thank You for protecting me. Thank You for such good friends who walk through life's journey with me." She stilled as a lump filled her throat. "Father, I don't understand why this happened. Help me to forgive and to move on..." There was nothing left to say. "Amen."

"Amen."

Neither woman moved.

"Thank you."

"My pleasure. You didn't think I'd let you leave without it, did you? Sorry there wasn't a full sermon about an ark. I'll see if I can't come up with one."

"Was I that heavy-handed last year?"

"A touch."

Tricia crinkled her nose and laughed. "I'm taking this coffee, and we have to move. You've got a job to do."

"Speaking of that, I want to do an interview with you. A chance to get your story out about Andrew Parker. I'll talk to Kate about it today."

"Will it make a difference?" Tricia didn't want to believe that all the bad publicity could be thwarted.

"It might and it can't hurt anything."

Tricia considered the ramifications a moment and then nodded. "All right, I'll give my best friend the scoop on what happened."

After Dani dropped her at her car, Tricia hurried into the office. Even if Sydney was taking over the Parker trial, she needed to order those files before she went anywhere else. As soon as the elevator opened, Tricia rushed into the hallway. She bounced off Charlie Francis.

"Tricia." He looked like he might give her a hug, then reconsidered. "I thought I told Sydney to tell you not to come in today. After yesterday, don't you need some time?"

"I need to pull a file, and double-check on the Parker case with Sydney."

He took her by the elbow and pulled her into a small conference room. She sank into a chair and braced for whatever was coming.

Charlie studied her. "We'll get the file pulled for you. And don't worry about the Parker case. Sydney will wrap it up tomorrow. The judge gave her today to get up to speed."

"I'll let her know she can call with questions."

Charlie leaned against the table and looked down at her. "I wish you'd told me about your history with Parker."

"I'm sorry. I wanted to believe it wouldn't be a factor."

"You still should have told me. You put our office in a precarious position. If Sydney hadn't worked alongside you, we might have had to drop the charges. There could still be ethics charges filed against you."

"Yes, sir." She knew what he said was right, but she'd wanted to believe none of that would happen.

He eased into a chair next to her. "Tricia, we'll work it out. The papers will mention it for a few days and then it'll blow over. We'll have to wait and see if there's any other fallout from your testimony. Take the rest of the week—more time if you need it—to take care of the things you need to do."

Tricia nodded. "Thank you."

"Next time, tell me ahead of time if there's any kind of conflict."

"I will." Tricia looked at him and waited. Was there more?

He studied her. "You sure you're okay?"

Tricia shrugged. "As well as I can be, considering everything that's happened."

"I'm glad for your sake it's out in the open. That was a very brave thing you did. I know Linda Parker appreciates it, too. Don't let this mire you down. We need you back here." He looked at his watch. "I've got a meeting, but let me know if there's anything you need." He got up and left without another word.

Tricia sat there a minute grateful for his concern, but hating it was necessary. Could he ever see her as the exceptional attorney without the fog of her past? She couldn't control that, so she needed to get to work. As she hurried to her office, sympathetic gazes followed her. Fortunately, most of her colleagues were on the phones or out of the office. She didn't know how much more compassion she could take before she broke down. Tears already tickled her eyes.

Once she reached her office, she shut and locked the door. Tricia sank into her chair and spun around. Someone knocked on the door, but she didn't get up. Whoever it was could wait or leave. She didn't care.

The knocking continued. With a sigh, Tricia pushed from her chair and opened the door.

Sydney stepped inside and hugged Tricia, warmth and acceptance flowing from her as her friend's delicate perfume tickled her nose. She released Tricia, who returned to her desk. "Tricia, I'm handling the Parker case. I thought you got my message."

"I did."

'Then why are you here?" Sydney settled onto the chair in front of Tricia's desk.

"Because I need to order the Lincoln Life fire file. The fire investigator has a theory that Caleb thinks has merit. But we need the information pulled from cold storage."

"You could have called. I would have handled that for you."

"I know." Fatigue washed over her, pushing her into the chair. "I needed to see for myself how Charlie would take seeing me."

"And?"

"He's disappointed that I didn't tell him about my history with Andrew, but he.. .he said I was brave. For taking the stand like that. I don't feel brave."

"He's a good man." Sydney squeezed her hand. "We can cover your files and cases for a few days. You need to take care of yourself. Find a place to live. Review the files if you think it will help."

Tricia filled Sydney in on the theory. "The connection seems to be that fire."

"Assuming that you're the reason your mom and Caleb had fires."

"Yes. But it makes sense. Each fire was more destructive than the ones before."

Sydney stood and headed to the door. "Maybe. I don't know whether to hope you're right or wrong. I'll get that file ordered. Promise me you'll be careful today, okay? If you're right, then the arsonist may not be done."

"All the more reason to get the suspects narrowed down." Tricia looked at the pile on her desk. "Do you think I should have forced the issue of the Parker case with Charlie?"

Sydney closed the office door and turned back to Tricia. "I don't know what I would have done if I'd been in your shoes. But everyone was blindsided by what happened yesterday. I didn't even know and had to jump in. I'm just glad I was there."

Tricia swallowed against the sudden lump in her throat. "Me, too."

Sydney gripped the back of the chair she'd vacated. "I understand why you didn't share your past with Parker, but Charlie needed to know. If nothing else, to be ready if, when, it somehow became a factor in the trial." Sydney's gaze overflowed with compassion as she studied Tricia. "For what it's worth, though, I think you're brave, too."

Tricia straightened in her seat. "Thanks."

As soon as Sydney left, Tricia got on the phone and called Caleb. She needed news. Preferably that the police had a suspect. A face and a name to go with the shadow that had tried to destroy her life.

"Tricia, I don't know what to tell you. We need your list." Caleb sounded bone weary. "Westmont should be here soon with Noah. Once they're here, we'll scour the list. Maybe they'll pick up on something I'm missing."

"Why is Noah with him?"

Caleb quickly filled her in, and she tried to hold back her frustration. "Is everyone I know going to be hurt in this?"

"He got the fire out before anything could happen." Caleb paused.

"If the text I got from Westmont is any indication, Noah thinks he's fine. The doctor seems to think he will be in a month or so." She could hear the amusement in his voice. "I'm surprised you haven't already talked to him."

She felt her cheeks flush, even though no one else was in the room. "Don't get distracted." Tricia wove the phone cord between her fingers. "We have to hurry, Caleb. Before the arsonist does something else."

"He could be done."

"It's possible, but I'm not buying it." Tricia sighed and pressed the phone against her ear. "I've ordered the file. Until it arrives, I'll review the electronic pleadings, see what I can find. And I'll let you know when the case file is ready."

The next hour passed in a flash. When Tricia looked up from the papers in front of her, it was after eleven. She now had a complete list of the people killed and injured in the fire. It was a starting point with more concrete information for the police to chase down. After printing out a couple of the pleadings to take with her, Tricia grabbed the papers and her purse and headed to the elevator. With Sydney taking care of the file, there was nothing else she could do here.

She'd emailed the list to Caleb, and now he and Westmont could chase down the names for possible leads. Her path to the elevator was slowed by several people stopping her to let her know they cared. The receptionist even made a point of hugging her.

"I've been praying for you." Her gray head bobbed with her words as if to reinforce them. "He'll carry you through this."

The words and friendship were a balm to her battered heart. "Thank you."

When the elevator doors opened and she stepped inside, she felt an odd swirl of relief over the grace her colleagues had extended to her, grief from all she had lost, and panic over all she had to do to piece her life back together.

22

T*uesday*

Noah hobbled around the conference room at the police station waiting for Westmont to come back with some coffee. He hoped it was better than the sludge he'd gotten at other stations around town. As soon as they'd arrived, Caleb had placed a call to Tricia. Seemed she was headed their way with the list of victims from the Lincoln Life fire.

While he waited for Westmont, his thoughts cycled back to the attorney he hoped to get to know a lot better. There was a spark even in the midst of so much loss that made Tricia special. He wanted to be there as she reconstructed her life, but he wasn't sure how to make it clear that he cared deeply about her and not just about keeping her safe.

Westmont walked into the room with one mug. "Here you go."

"Where's yours?"

Westmont placed the mug with a couple packets of sugar and creamer on the table next to Noah. "I'm not risking it. How desperate are you?"

"For caffeine?" Noah took a sip and grimaced. "Not sure I'm this desperate." He dumped a sugar packet in it. Slightly better—at least it was barely drinkable now.

"I'll be back." Westmont disappeared through the door without another word, leaving Noah to the room.

Noah settled into the chair and let his mind spin with ideas. Tricia would need to take things slowly, but he had no problem with that. What woman didn't like to be wooed? He didn't have lots of experience with women, but Noah wanted his first attempt with Tricia to succeed. The guys at the fire station who planned their approach seemed to end up with greater success than the ones who expected women to fall at their feet.

The thought of Tricia Jamison throwing herself at his feet made him cough up coffee. He could think of when that event would happen. Sometime between never and eternity.

Instead, he'd get her a dozen roses and take her to Grisanti's or the Green Gateau. Show her he valued her. And then, once his leg healed again, take her on a date that showed her what he was like. Cross-country skiing. Hiking trails. Canoeing. Let her see his heart.

Did he love Tricia?

Sure, he found her beautiful. Who wouldn't, with those incredible brown eyes and a beauty that radiated from the inside as well as the outside? Her mind never stopped and neither did her heart. She still had such compassion for people in need, in spite of her past, maybe because of it.

He rubbed his neck and propped his leg up on a chair. His knee throbbed. The kind of pain he could ignore while concentrating on something else, but the kind that pulsed a steady beat when undistracted, as he was now. Did Tricia's past exert the same effect on her? She didn't have tape around her knee or a limp in her stride to alert the rest of the world to her pain. But did the painful memories throb through her days and nights?

He doubted that he could have survived everything she had. Not without the grace and strength that flowed straight from God's throne room.

Did he have the right to ask her these questions yet?

He sat there and prayed about how best to aid Tricia without pushing her away. This wasn't something he could fix even if all he wanted to do was punch the men who had hurt her.

The door swung open and bounced off the wall. Westmont and Jamison entered the room. Westmont wore a sheepish look, almost as if he'd rather be on patrol duty than back in here. Jamison looked like he'd reached the end of his rope. Noah braced himself for whatever was about to hit.

Caleb pulled out a chair across the table and straddled it. "Tricia faxed her list."

Silence settled on the room, then Westmont shifted against the wall. A knock sounded at the door. Westmont opened it. Weary strode into the room, and Noah jerked to attention.

Weary sat down next to Noah. "All right, boys. Now that we've got that list, let's get down to business. We still have an arsonist to find. The prosecutor's office told me Tricia called for the boxes, and I've been promised that we'll have them later today. Your theory is the best one so far, Brust. I've asked the police to help us track down the activities of the victims' families or significant others during the last twenty-four hours. We'll move backward if needed."

Caleb leaned back in his chair. "We've got investigators working under Denimore to I.D. where as many of them were yesterday before the fire as we can. It'll take at least a day to get preliminary reports back. They all know it's a priority."

"When those files are uncovered, I want to know about it. And I want you involved in reviewing them, Brust. You were at the fire. And I think you'll be able to add important details to the paper record."

Noah nodded. He had no intention of being anywhere else. "Does this mean I'm back on the investigation?"

"No. Technically you're on paid leave due to that knee of yours. What you do with your paid leave is your business."

"That's easy. I'll be right here as long as Caleb will let me stay, or with Tricia."

Weary rolled his eyes. "Get to work."

AT A STOPLIGHT, Tricia scanned the list of names. All were vaguely familiar from the trial, but a year had passed. Enough time to forget many of the details associated with the names. At the end of the list she saw two names. Brothers? Father and son? Evan Gillmore. Timothy Gillmore.

Tricia stilled. Why did that last name ring a bell?

The light turned green, and Tricia stuffed the sheet in her purse. She hoped Caleb or Noah found something as they reviewed the list. That the arsonist had slipped up and left them something to work with. Somewhere the clue existed that would break the case wide open. She knew that to the core of who she was.

Tricia's cell phone rang, and she picked it up from the console. "Hello."

"Hey, sweetie." Mom sounded subdued. "I went through the closet in your old room and pulled some clothes for you."

Tricia smiled. The clothes might be a bit dated—no, classic—but they would help tide her over while she rebuilt her wardrobe, and her life. "Thank you. That will be a great help." She looked at the clock. Shortly after noon. Better to do this now while Frank was at work. "Is it okay if I swing by now to pick them up?"

Mom hesitated a moment. "Yes, I'll be here for a bit. Have you eaten?"

"No. Hadn't really thought about food."

"Then I'll pull together a light lunch for us."

"Great. I'll be there in a few minutes."

At the next intersection Tricia turned the car down the street that would eventually wind back to her mother's home. As she drove, she marveled at the sense of freedom that seemed to follow her.

Yes, in the last week her most deeply hidden secrets and pain had been exposed. First, telling Caleb about Frank. Then, the revelations about Andrew yesterday. Part of her had feared feeling exposed and violated by the revelations. Instead, it felt like the burden of hidden shame had eased. Had the past lost some of its hold in the unveiling, in the pulling her secrets into the light? And if so, should she expose everything Frank had done? Tell Mom what had happened all those nights she'd traveled for work?

It seemed like the time. But she wanted to do this the right way. In a way that brought healing, peace, maybe even restoration to their relationship.

She parked and took a moment to catch her breath. Lord, I need You. Show me if this is the time. And guide the conversation. Turn this into something good. Please.

Tricia climbed from the car and walked to the door. The only hint of flames came from the vibrant red leaves of the maple at the side of the front yard. Tricia knocked on the door then opened it.

She followed the sounds of clanging pans to the kitchen. "I thought you were making a light lunch."

"You know how it is." Mom looked up from the stove, wisps of hair framing her face in twists and curls. "One thing leads to another." The woman flitted around the kitchen as if she couldn't sit still. Tricia watched her, concern creeping in. Mom only acted like this when something was bothering her.

"Everything okay, Mom?"

Her mom flicked a hand in the air. "We should talk about you." She wiped her hands on her pants and turned to look at Tricia. She opened her arms and pulled Tricia into a hug. "How are you?"

Tricia let the hug settle over her, inhaling the faint scent of Mom's orchid body spray. "Losing my house probably hasn't settled in yet. Hope you still have copies of all those photos."

"Of course. That's what a pack-rat mother is for."

Tricia laughed. The basement did contain every scrap of paper she'd ever doodled on and each award she'd received. "Thanks for thinking to pull together those clothes for me."

A shadow fell across Mom's face. She turned down the temperature on the stove. A premonition of something pulsed through Tricia. "Speaking of that. When I pulled out clothes, this fell off the shelf." Mom picked up a thin, spiral-bound volume from the counter. How had Tricia missed that?

She reached for it, fingers stroking the cover of the journal she'd filled with her fear and anger during the period when Frank had molested her. It had been a safe place to pour her hurt while Caleb was consumed with college and Mom had been blinded to the other side of Frank.

Tricia swallowed, wondering what to say.

"Is it true?"

Tricia blinked and looked at Mom. "What?"

"The things you wrote about Frank? Are they true?" Mom's voice rose with a hysterical note in it.

"Yes."

What little color she'd had drained from her mother's face, leaving her complexion pasty. She backed up to the table and collapsed onto a chair. "Why didn't you ever say anything? Come to me?"

"I wanted to..." Oh, how she'd wanted to. "But, Mama, every time you looked at Frank, you saw a hero. And he told me he'd make sure you never believed me." Tricia took a breath, and prayed for wisdom. "I tried to say something a couple times, but the words would never come. I was so ashamed. How could I tell anyone my stepfather would come into my room and...forced himself on me?"

A sob escaped from Mom's clamped lips. "I'm so sorry." Tears coursed down her cheeks. "I knew something was wrong. But I didn't make you talk to me. I wanted to pretend everything was okay. That we were a happy family. Even though it felt as if you'd left, even while you lived here."

The words stung, cutting at Tricia's heart. Her mom had known something was wrong? She wanted to demand to know why she hadn't pushed, why she'd never been willing to confront the truth of what happened. Could Tricia move beyond the past without... what? What did she want from her mom? Acknowledgment that the horror had happened? An apology for not stopping it?

Father? It felt like someone was holding her, sheltering her, and assuring her she was loved and always had been. She closed her eyes and soaked in the love. *Thank You, Father.*

Her daddy may have died, and her stepfather...well, he'd never been a father to her. But she knew with certainty that her Heavenly Father had seen it all. Walked through every night, every moment with her. She'd never been alone, even as she felt abandoned. Maybe she'd never understand why God had allowed the horrors, but she could choose to accept His love and commit to moving forward into the future.

Tricia opened her eyes. "Mom, I will let you decide what to do about Frank. He's your husband. Understand that I will never choose to be near the man. But I am trying hard to forgive and move forward."

Mom gave her a teary smile. Her fingers played with her necklace. "I don't know what to do."

"I can't tell you. But you need to know the true heart of the man you chose to marry." Tricia opened the journal and scanned an entry. "I'm just sorry you had to learn about it this way."

Mom nodded. She opened her mouth, then cleared her throat. She leaned forward and looked into Tricia's eyes. Tricia could see hurt warring with fear and anger. "Sweetie, forgive me for not protecting you. For not asking the hard questions because I was afraid."

Tricia considered her words. She didn't want to say the right words without meaning them. As she examined her heart though, she found that she did forgive her mom. What a transformation in a week. "I forgive you. Mom, I love you."

The two women hugged, and Tricia felt a bridge between them for the first time in more than a dozen years. Tears mingled on their cheeks as the past lost its power in the light of day.

The smoke detector shrieked, and the women startled. Mom jumped to her feet and scurried to the stove. "Oh, my. Guess I forgot our lunch."

Tricia laughed as she dragged a chair over to the smoke detector and turned it off. Once the alarm was silenced, she pushed the chair back to the table. A card caught her eye. It was addressed to Evan Gillmore, who lived one street over from Mom. It needed a stamp.

Evan Gillmore, from the Lincoln Life trial, lived only a block away from her mom? Was that why the name had seemed familiar when she saw it on the list?

"Mom?" She held up the card. "What's this for?"

"Such a tragedy," Mom answered, shaking her head as she bustled around the kitchen. "His son died just over a week ago. Little Timmy was just six years old."

Tricia clutched the back of the chair in front of her as her knees went weak. *That* was where she'd seen the name before. She'd read about him in the paper: how Timmy had been injured in the Lincoln Life fire, falling into a coma from which he'd never awakened, his body horribly burned.

She remembered seeing the obituary...the morning after the fire at her mother's.

This was it—the key, the connection they'd scoured every file and record to find. Tricia had just uncovered it, on her mother's kitchen table.

23

Tuesday

Noah stared at the sheets of paper spread across the table, struggling to read the list of names. He ran a finger down the injured list. Wait a minute.

Timothy Gillmore.

"Hey, Caleb. Wasn't Timothy Gillmore a kid injured in the fire? I know I've seen this name recently. In the last week or so."

Caleb scratched his neck, then stretched in his chair. "Yeah, I think so. There was only one kid injured, right?"

"That I remember." That time was dominated by the death of his father in his mind.

Westmont looked up from the computer in the corner. He tapped a few keys. "This article lists one kid, Timothy Gillmore, age four. According to the *Journal,* he'd visited the office with his dad for a meeting. His father, Evan, was also injured, but both survived. At least initially."

Noah stood and hobbled over to look at the article. Westmont leaned to the side and Noah scanned it. Time slowed as he began to piece the elements together. "Didn't one of the survivors die a week ago?"

Westmont did another search and pulled up an obituary.

"Yep, here it is." Noah stared at the photo of a cute little boy. How it must hurt to lose him after watching him suffer for a year. "He died less than two weeks ago. What do you want to bet that would push the dad to act?"

Caleb nodded. Noah could almost see the wheels spinning in his mind. Caleb pulled the phone on the table in front of him. "It's game time. Let's bring Mr. Gillmore in for a conversation."

While Caleb made his call, Noah continued to read the article.

Westmont sighed. "You gonna be much longer?"

Noah refused to be hurried, not on something this important. As he read, pieces clicked into place. He reread the sentence. Why hadn't he thought of that before? Where was that list? "Westmont, where's that list with the partial license plate matches?"

Westmont handed him a document and watched as Noah scanned it. "That's it. There's another connection."

Westmont and Jamison looked at him, questions filling their faces.

"Remember the partial license plate number of the vehicle that hit Jessie?"

Caleb nodded. "018."

A smile spread across Westmont's face. "You found it?"

"Yep. Look here. One of the cars with that partial is owned by an Evan Gillmore. I doubt that there are many Evan Gillmores in the area."

Noah didn't feel satisfaction as it all clicked into place. "Yet another thing to ask Gillmore about when you bring him in."

Caleb looked at Westmont. "Get the address from DMV."

"Will do." Westmont sprang to his feet and headed to the door.

Noah watched him go with mixed feelings. It was too early to celebrate, especially since they didn't have the guy yet. And he didn't like the idea that the man had reacted to his son's death in this way. Unfortunately it gave him a viable reason for snapping. "Is this enough to nail the guy?"

Caleb shook his head. "Probably not. But it's enough to apply pressure and see if he'll confess. I've found guilty parties often itch to confess. They just don't know it. Stay here while Westmont and I chase a few things down. You can rest. We'll be back when we have more info."

"All right." Something bugged him about their line of thought. Just because the man's son had died didn't explain why he'd start fires at Caleb's and Tricia's. There was more going on, but what was elusive. Noah settled back in his chair. He might have a bum knee, but that didn't mean he couldn't keep working. Westmont had left the computer open, so Noah poked around the paper's website looking for more info. His phone rang as he read.

"Brust."

"Noah?" Tricia's voice sounded tight and far away.

"Yep."

"I found something. Gillmore..."

He tucked the phone tighter to his ear. "What? Tricia?" Silence answered. He pulled the phone from his ear, checked the bars for service. He should still hear her. But the line had turned eerily silent. "Tricia, where are you? Tricia?"

Westmont hurried back into the room. "I've got the address from DMV. I'm headed out there with another officer."

Noah turned from the phone, wanting to hurl it against the wall. "Let me know when you have him."

"I will." Westmont studied him. "What's wrong?"

"Tricia called but we got disconnected as you came in."

"Call her back." The guy said it as if it was the most logical next step in the world.

"I haven't had a chance."

A buzzing sound filled the room, and Westmont looked down at his pager. Whatever flashed across the screen wasn't good because the man tore out of the office at a sprint. A minute later, Caleb ran in. He tossed some keys at Noah.

"My car's the blue Accord in the left corner. Take it wherever you need to go."

"Where are you headed?"

"Police business. I'll call you when I need the car again." Caleb scooted back out the door.

Noah stared at the keys. He needed the wheels, but first he had some questions to answer about Evan Gillmore. He also didn't like that Tricia's call had been disconnected. It probably meant nothing more than a dead zone, but after this week, he wanted to be sure. He dialed her number and waited as it rang. After several rings, the mechanical recording of her voice mail kicked in.

"Tricia, this is Noah. Call me. I'm worried about losing your call. I'm at the police station but Caleb and Westmont tore out of here a moment ago. I'm headed out to Caleb's car. Evan Gillmore looks like our man. His son died recently from complications from injuries he sustained in the fire. Evan was injured in the fire, too. Call me." Noah wanted to continue but the voice-mail system cut him off.

As he waited for her to call him back, Noah grabbed the phone book and flipped to the Gs. While a few Gillmores were listed, none were an *E* or *Evan.* He hoped DMV's address for Evan was still valid. He tried Tricia once more. A bad feeling settled in his gut when it again tripped over to voicemail.

24

T*uesday*

Dead. It figured. Right when Tricia needed it, her cell battery gave up. She'd head home, but she had no home. She didn't even own a charger anymore. It had turned to melted plastic, burned in the fire, along with her other possessions. One more thing to add to her massive list of items she had to replace.

Mom hurried down the hallway with two suitcases.

"Are there any more in the bedroom?" Tricia reached for one of the cases.

"No." Mom released the handle, then brushed her bangs out of her eyes. "When you decide where you're living, I'll go through towels, sheets and other things you'll need."

"Clothes are a great start."

They walked to the Miata and wrestled the suitcases into the tiny car. Tricia had to laugh after she wedged the second into place. "Maybe it's a good thing this is all for now."

Mom nodded. "Tricia, I'm sorry about everything."

"It's in the past and forgiven." Tricia hugged her and they walked back to the house. "Can I borrow your cell phone? Mine just died."

"Sure." Mom pulled it out of her purse and the charger out of the junk drawer. "Let me know if you need anything else." Tricia thanked her and headed down the sidewalk. An acrid smell tickled her nose. A fire? She scanned the area, but didn't see smoke. She should call Noah back, let him know she had a new number if he needed to get hold of her. What was his number? She dialed in the one she hoped was right.

He answered on the first ring. "Where are you, Tricia?"

"Getting ready to leave Mom's and head to Southpointe to start replacing some of the things I lost. Has anything happened?"

"Caleb and Westmont are zeroing in on Evan Gillmore."

"His son just died." It all made sense with that piece falling into place.

"Yep."

Tricia reached her car and started juggling the keys out of her purse. She felt a sharp poke in her back and stopped. "Noah, I wanted to let you know I don't have..."

Her words died in her throat when she caught a glimpse of a hooded man standing a step behind her with a gun shoved in her back in the car's side mirror.

"End the call." His words sounded hoarse, like he'd inhaled too much smoke at some point and his vocal chords hadn't recovered.

"Noah..." The gun dug deeper into her flesh. She hit the button to disconnect the call. She slid the phone into her pocket. "Who are you?"

"Get in the car, Miss Jamison. We're going for a drive."

She hesitated. He knew her name? Tricia looked around, searching for a way out, but no options presented themselves. She didn't have any choice but to obey. Mom wouldn't hear her in the house. No one was outside doing yard work. And she'd ended the call. Now she had to make him forget she still had the phone so she could hit redial without being noticed.

"Do anything funny while I'm going around the car and I'll shoot." The man looked like he would do it.

She studied him, even as she plotted a way out.

If she hurried, maybe she could get the car in gear before he got around and climbed in the passenger seat. She pulled her keys from her purse, then slid into the car. As soon as she hit the seat, she scrambled to hit the locks, but he'd already opened his door. Maybe she could get the car moving before he got all the way in. She shoved the key in the ignition, turned the key and heard the engine catch. Her hand touched the gearshift. A muffled shot pierced the sky, and she jumped.

He slid in, gun pointed at her head. "I told you—nothing funny."

Tricia's heart pounded. Maybe someone had heard the shot. Could she stall long enough for help to arrive?

The man collapsed his frame into the passenger seat, and the small car shook. "Now you can roll."

She watched the houses around her. Nobody had come out. Was *Oprah* so interesting that no one noticed the gunshot? Her throat tightened and she struggled to breathe. Would anyone find her if she followed his orders? And if she didn't, would he shoot her? She wanted to fight back, but she also wanted to live. *Help me!*

He'd almost folded in half to fit. The red sweatshirt hood cloaked his face even further as he kept his gaze forward. Still the gun never wavered from pointing at her ribs. Could this be Evan Gillmore?

That was crazy. He hadn't been on her radar until Noah mentioned him a few minutes ago. It wasn't like that would be enough to conjure him to her car.

"Move." The word was accompanied by a jab, and she jolted.

Her hand trembled on the gearshift. He waved the gun, and she pulled the gearshift into Drive. She barely pushed the gas pedal, letting the car crawl from the curb to the road.

"Now what?"

"Drive." He settled back against the seat, the corner of a suitcase poking the back of his head.

She itched to reach into her pocket and play with her phone. No, couldn't do it yet. Not when his eyes never left her. The man had a hyperalert look, one that told Tricia he wouldn't miss anything. When they reached the next intersection, he gave her a quiet instruction to turn.

"Do I get to know who you are?" Her voice quivered.

"You were part of my worst nightmare. Now I'm yours."

It unnerved her that he knew her, when she was sure she'd never seen him. After everything she'd survived this week, Tricia refused to become a statistic now. She'd overcome too much. Get him talking. She had to do something. "What's your name?"

He stared at her, but he wouldn't say anything. She kept her eyes on the road until the next red light, then turned to him. "Please, tell me something. Why are you doing this?" With a halting motion, he rolled up one of his sweatshirt sleeves while keeping the gun trained on her. Her gaze dropped to his arm. Took in the mottled and wavy pattern to the skin. Bums?

Could it be?

~

NOAH TURNED onto another side street and approached Mrs. Randol's house. He wasn't waiting for Tricia to call him back this time. The cut-off call worried him, and he needed to know she was all right.

His phone vibrated, and he pulled it from its holder. "Brust."

"There's another fire." Weary's voice charged with energy. "This one could be tied to the others. Meet me there."

"What's the address?" Noah pulled over and wrote it down, his heart accelerating when he realized it was a block from Mrs. Randol's house. Was Tricia there? Could the fire be the reason she'd ended the call? "I can be there in ten minutes."

As soon as the call ended, Noah whipped the car back onto the road, driving faster now. Once he reached 70th, Noah headed north a couple of miles then turned into the neighborhood. Billowing smoke provided an eerily accurate way to identify the correct house. Flames fully engulfed the structure when he pulled to a stop several houses back.

Noah stepped from his truck and started looking for a group of investigators amid the spectators. He scanned those watching across the street, but none of them looked familiar. A mix of horror and fascination stained their faces, as the flames reflected in their expressions. Noah didn't think he'd seen them at the earlier fires, but at this point in the investigation he didn't expect to. Nothing else had gone as expected, even if Weary suspected this fire might be tied to the others.

A waving hand caught his attention. Weary stood next to Jamison and Westmont. Noah made his way over, spiders of knowing crawling around his gut.

"Nice of you to join us, Brust." Caleb's words didn't match his sober expression.

Noah gestured at the house. "What brought you two here?"

"This house belongs to Evan Gillmore." Westmont paused, letting the words settle. "Neighbors called 911, complaining they thought they'd heard a gunshot about half an hour ago. By the time the patrol car arrived, flames were everywhere."

Evan Gillmore. But why a fire at his own house? An explosion made the four men duck. Noah watched the flames lick the sky, hungrily searching for fuel. "It's running out."

Caleb looked at him like he'd gone crazy. "That fire? Running out of what? It's destroying the house: Leaving nothing behind."

"It's looking for fuel. Any chance Gillmore's in there?" He pointed with his chin.

Caleb shrugged. "There was a gunshot, and now there's a fire. Anyone seen a body?"

Westmont shrugged. "Not that we know of."

"It doesn't smell like there's one." Weary's mouth was set in a determined line. "If there was a body, I guarantee you'd smell it."

Noah nodded, the foul aroma one he'd never forget.

Caleb looked at his watch. "Anyone heard from Tricia lately?"

"We got cut off in the middle of a conversation a bit ago. She hasn't returned the call. I was headed this way to check on her." Noah couldn't ignore the unease he felt. "I don't like

that she's out there by herself." Noah looked beyond the house to the ones behind it. "Caleb, that's your mom's house, right?"

"Yes." He squinted as if trying to see through the smoke. "Looks like Mom's in the backyard. I'll go see if she's heard from Tricia." The man hurried across a neighbor's yard.

Noah considered following, but decided against it. He turned to Weary. "Anything else we can do here?"

Firefighters kept water trained on the home, but the flames hadn't begun to burn down. Noah estimated it would take at least another hour to get it under control. Another hour or more before they could explore the shell.

Weary shook his head. "It's a waiting game."

"Brust!"

Noah tried to find the source of the voice. Jamison ran toward him.

"Come on. Tricia was at Mom's. She's got Mom's cell but isn't answering. Mom thought she saw her talking to someone, but got distracted by the fire. When she went back to the front yard to wave, Tricia had pulled away."

The bad feeling was back. They had to reach Tricia. "What's your mom's number?" Maybe he'd stored it incorrectly. Noah entered it as Caleb relayed it. He paced as he waited for it to ring. Then waited for her to answer. Instead, it kicked over to voice mail. He tried again, but this time nothing. Caleb sucked in a breath. "I didn't tell you the bad part." Noah braced.

"She wasn't alone in the car."

25

T*uesday*

Tricia jumped as the phone rang. So much for the mystery man—Evan Gillmore—forgetting about the phone.

"Hand it over."

"I can't reach it. It's in my pocket."

He snapped his fingers, and she fumbled with the seat belt. The car swerved around the road as she tried to tug it from her jeans' pocket. "Can I wait till we're at a stoplight?"

"Don't try anything funny."

Tricia looked forward and tried to think where the Talk button was. She slid her fingers across the screen, hoping she'd hit the right place to accept the call. This had to work or no one would know anything was wrong. She prayed the caller was Noah or Caleb, but only Noah knew she had this phone. She prayed it wasn't someone calling for her mom. She needed help, and Noah was her only option.

She placed both hands on the steering wheel and hoped he'd forget about the phone. "Who are you?"

"A man whose life was destroyed by you."

Tricia stole another look at him. "I don't know what you think I did."

Menace filled his glare. "You got the fire department off the hook for the fire."

"The Lincoln Life fire?" He nodded, and her suspicions were confirmed. "Evan Gillmore."

"So you're as smart as you look."

If only she'd done a better job of figuring it out. "Why me? I wasn't lead counsel on that case."

"I watched every day of that trial. The jury was siding with us, the victims. Then you got up there and started twisting things around. The jury lost focus. And when they accepted your arguments, we lost."

How could she make him see reality? She'd played such a small role in the overall case. Including Noah, she'd only handled a few witnesses. She hadn't even made the opening or closing argument. Then she glanced at him again. Judging by the crazed look in his eye, there was little she could say to reason with him.

"Turn right here."

She followed his instruction and pulled onto O Street. "Are we headed downtown?"

"I've got big plans for you. Too bad you couldn't have been caught in the fire at your house. But there's poetic justice in where you will die."

Traffic slowed in front of her as one of the many lights on O turned red.

"Hand over the phone." He held his empty hand out, waving the gun with the other. "You didn't think I forgot."

Tricia unfastened her seat belt, scrambling for any way to hang on to the phone longer. He waved the gun, and she tugged it out with a quick glance at the screen. She couldn't tell if her call had gone through. Even if she had succeeded, the act of freeing it had turned it off.

His choice of words played in her mind. Poetic justice? If they continued on this course, they'd be downtown in less than ten minutes. What did he have in mind? She searched the skyline. A construction crane stood in stark relief against the clear sky. The shell of the new Lincoln Life site looked empty.

"The Lincoln Life site?"

"You are smart." Admiration tinged his words. "Too bad nobody will find you until it's too late. Quit stalling and give me the phone."

She held it in her hand, wanting to keep it and the chance for help it offered. He ripped the phone from her and tucked it in his jacket.

"I hope your faith in the fire department is well placed. We're about to give them a test. You're the bait."

~

NOAH PRESSED his phone to his ear. At first he'd thought there was no one on the other end, but soon he could faintly make out voices. He motioned to the others to quiet down. Words filtered through the phone in a static, garbled fashion. It was as if something were covering the mouthpiece, muffling the words.

"Caleb, I think this might be Tricia and whoever has her."

Caleb pulled a small notepad from his pocket and a pen. "Write down anything we need to know."

Noah nodded, then tossed Caleb his keys. "Let's get mobile in case we're needed."

Caleb led the way to the vehicle, with Westmont behind him. Noah brought up the rear as he limped to the car. Would his voice carry to the other end if he relayed what he heard? He hit the Mute button, and prayed that worked. He slid into the backseat, then cupped both ears trying to follow the muffled conversation.

"He just admitted he's Gillmore."

Westmont turned to look at Noah. "Looks like you were right."

"So our theory is confirmed. But where is he taking her?" Caleb smacked the steering wheel. "We have to find them. Fast. Call the station. See if they can do any kind of triangulation on Mom's phone."

"Why not GPS?" That seemed like a faster solution to Noah.

"Mom's phone is too old to hope for that type of technology." Caleb started the car and pulled onto the street. He caught Noah's gaze in the rearview mirror. "Get me information on where they're headed. I'll take general directions at this point."

Noah nodded. That was his top priority. He tried to tune out Westmont as he talked to the fire station on his cell. What was Tricia feeling as she drove around town with the man who had destroyed her home and kidnapped her?

Poetic justice? Is that what Gillmore just said?

"Caleb, head downtown." He wasn't sure what the man meant, but downtown had to be the right area, since that's where the Lincoln Life fire had occurred. He needed more to go on.

At the next intersection Caleb obeyed, but Noah's attention was on the suddenly silent phone pressed to his ear. Nothing. He pulled it away to look at the screen. The connection was gone. He wanted to throw the phone against the windshield.

How could he find her now?

"Caleb, hurry. The call got cut off. We've got to find them."

Caleb flipped on his lights, and the car jumped ahead. Noah held his breath and prayed. Somehow they had to find her before Gillmore harmed her.

26

Tuesday

The Lincoln Life building loomed in front of them.

"This is where my son's life should have ended."

Tricia looked at the building, trying to remember what the old one had looked like. Imagined the flames consuming the building as it had on that terrible day. She'd watched the flames from her office and prayed for all the people in the building. So many had escaped unharmed. But not all.

"Timothy survived."

Gillmore snorted. "If you can call that living. He never left the hospital. You can't imagine the horror of watching your son's skin melt. Hearing his screams, begging you to make it stop." He pointed to an area to the left of the building. "Pull in there."

A sign designated it *Construction Only*, but Gillmore forced her to get out of the car and lead him into the building.

"That day was a lot like this one. His preschool was closed so he got to run a few errands with me. Then I'd promised him a picnic at a park. We'd get a Happy Meal, and he could run and swing."

Tricia pulled the door, hoping it would be locked, but it opened. The inside still looked like a shell. Stacks of sheetrock piled next to rolls of carpet. Her heels clicked against the concrete floor as he urged her along the floor toward the elevator bank.

"We were only stopping here long enough to drop off the application and a check to a buddy. He worked on the third floor. By the time the fire alarm went off, the elevators were locked down. And the doors to the stairwells wouldn't budge. In all the smoke, Timothy slipped from my grasp." He sucked in a ragged breath and pushed the button.

The elevator dinged and the doors glided open. Tricia looked around, but couldn't see anyone.

"No one is here to save you. That will be up to the fire department. We'll see if the fire department that couldn't save my son can find you in time." He pushed her into the elevator then punched the fifth floor.

"I found him, but not in time. And by the time the firefighters found us, his lungs had been scarred, in addition to all those bums on his skin. Timothy fought hard, but he never had a chance."

The doors opened, and he pushed her out.

Tricia stumbled, and used the diversion to look for anyone.

With all the construction, how had he managed to get her here when there was no one around? The floor was empty except for support pillars and random assortments of construction equipment. Even if she could get away from him, there was nowhere for her to hide. She'd be a sitting duck for him to shoot.

God, help me.

All she wanted to do was live through this. Hug her family and tell Noah how much she cared for him. She wanted a relationship. Wanted to let him into her heart. Build a future with him.

But to do that she had to survive.

"Don't do it." Gillmore jammed the gun against her head. "I'd rather not shoot you, but frankly I have nothing to lose. My wife left me after the fire. She couldn't stop blaming me for what happened to Timothy. And now Timothy's dead."

"I'm so sorry." He might not believe her, but she had to try. "I saw the obituary last week. My heart cried for your loss."

"But you didn't come. Nobody came to the funeral for the little boy who was forgotten." His voice hardened, the words falling as if chipped from the state capitol's tower. "Now we'll see if they remember you."

~

CALEB PULLED over in a parking lot near 27th and O. Noah thought he might go crazy with the waiting. Tricia was out there somewhere, needing them. Now. And all he could do was sit here, while she was at the mercy of a man bent on destroying her.

He did not like those odds.

"Thanks, Denimore." Westmont pumped his fist and turned to Noah. "He must not have turned the phone off. We've got a triangulation. They're near the corner of 16th and the Parkway."

Caleb tore out of the parking lot back onto O with his lights flashing and siren blaring. "Is Denimore headed there?"

"He's already got squad cars reporting to that area. They'll meet us there."

Noah's gaze roamed over downtown. Sixteenth and the Parkway. "Isn't that where the Lincoln Life building is going up?" Poetic justice. "That's it. He's going to do something to her there." Noah pulled his phone out and keyed in Weary's number. "He's taken her to the Lincoln Life building. He said something about poetic justice, so I think he plans to burn it down. Can you get some trucks to meet us there?"

Weary promised to move on it. Noah watched as Caleb zipped through intersection after intersection. He knew Caleb was driving as fast as possible, but it still felt like they would never reach the site in time. And what if they were wrong? What if Gillmore had ditched the phone or planted it to lure them off course? There might not be enough time left to find Tricia after figuring out the ruse.

The thought turned his stomach. He'd promised to protect her, and he was reduced to praying they'd find her in time.

"HERE WE GO." Gillmore pushed her to a pillar in the center of the floor. Next to it was a pile. Rope. Gas can. Matches.

Tricia's mouth went dry as she looked at the assembled items. There was no doubt that he planned to leave her here. Her gaze darted around. She had to get away from him before he could tie her up. She pushed away. Tried to run, but her shoes couldn't get traction on the slick concrete.

A bullet whizzed past her ear, pulling her up short.

"Next time I won't miss." His voice had a steely edge that communicated his resolve. "You can either cooperate and pray the firemen arrive in time. Or I can shoot you. It doesn't matter to me which you choose."

"I'll cooperate." When he put it like that, she had no choice.

He had her sit on the floor with her back to the pillar, then ordered her to lace her fingers behind it. He bound her wrists tightly with the rope, then stepped back. "I've already drenched the perimeter with gasoline. It won't take long to burn, but if the fire department responds quickly, you'll have a fighting chance. That's more than Timothy had."

Gillmore tucked the gun in his waistband, then picked up the box of matches and the gas can. With a quick salute he opened the can and began sloshing gasoline ten feet from her. He poured it as he walked to the elevator.

The elevator opened and he stepped inside. He struck a match, looked at her and threw the match.

"Good luck."

The spark found gasoline, which erupted into flames.

"ISN'T THAT TRICIA'S CAR?" Noah pointed to a parking lot beside the building where a Miata pulled away from the building.

Caleb tried to get into the lot, but had to wait for someone who was leaving. "That must be him. Westmont..."

"On it." Westmont already had his cell phone at his ear. In moments he gave a description of the car to the dispatcher.

Noah didn't wait for the rest of the call. Tricia had to be somewhere in that building. He looked up and noticed smoke billowing against the windows. The roar of sirens pulsed through the air as fire trucks pulled up to the scene.

"Brust, what are you doing here?" Graham yelled over the noise as he raced from the truck.

"Looking for someone special."

"Here." Graham threw a turnout coat at him. "There should be extra boots and pants in the jump seat, too."

Noah hurried over as fast as he could.

"What do we know about the scene?"

Noah yanked on the pants and boots. "We got here a minute before you did. Based on the other fires, I'm guessing gasoline or another accelerant was used. The arsonist also sees this as some type of test for us." Noah stepped closer and lowered his voice. "We can't fail this one, Graham. My girlfriend is inside."

Men attached hoses to fire hydrants and started running the hoses toward the building.

Graham grabbed his gear. "Let's go."

Noah hauled an oxygen tank on, then prepared to follow the others in.

Caleb ran beside him. "Find her and get her out of there." Noah nodded, concentrating on ignoring the pain in his knee. He'd have to be careful. He wouldn't do anyone any good if he had to be rescued. Graham had assigned men to each floor and each team headed to the stairwell.

His friend looked at Noah. "You and me, Brust. We've got the fifth floor."

That was a lot of stairs, but Noah gritted his teeth and climbed. As they passed each floor, it became clear Gillmore had stopped long enough to start fires at each level. The black smoke cloaked each floor, but without offices, cubicles and furniture to clutter the areas, the sweeps should proceed quickly. He prayed they were fast enough.

Finally, they reached the fifth floor. Noah heaved in oxygen, and Graham looked at him through his mask.

"Are you up to this?"

Noah nodded. He had to be.

Graham pounded through the door, Noah a step behind him. Flames were eating through stacks of sheetrock and climbing the outside walls. The air quality was poor. If Tricia was here, they had to find her and get her out now.

The further they moved into the floor, the harder it was to see and the more it seemed like the first Lincoln Life blaze. Flashes of that fire stopped Noah. He heard a voice, choking and calling for help. His dad?

Noah shook his head, tried to knock the memory aside. He couldn't get lost in the past. Couldn't relive that nightmare again. Not now. Tricia needed him. Needed every skill he'd developed and honed as a firefighter. Noah stumbled against the wall and fell to his knee. He groaned as pain shot up his leg.

God, help me. I can't do this on my own, but Tricia needs me. He could do this. He had to.

Graham shook his shoulder. "This way."

They dropped to the floor and crawled under the smoke. Noah let his arms do most of the work, scanning the area as he went.

Finally he spotted something ahead of him.

He elbowed Graham. Shoes. Clearly a lady's.

They triple-timed it her direction. Tricia's eyes were closed, her breathing shallow. How could that animal have done this to her? Rage flashed through Noah as he pulled his mask off long enough to start buddy-breathing with her.

Graham cut the rope holding her in place. She moaned as her arms dropped. Graham scooped her up while Noah stumbled to his feet.

"I've got her." Noah reached for her. He needed to do this.

Graham eyed him for a moment, then released his hold. "We've got to hurry."

Together they hurried to the door, then to the stairwell. The smoke had filtered into the stairwell, but the air there was still much cleaner. Noah rested a moment, then started the march down the stairs. Graham radioed ahead that they'd found Tricia.

When they reached the front doors, Caleb was waiting, along with paramedics who took Tricia from Noah.

"She's alive?" Worry hooded Caleb's eyes.

Noah nodded. They'd beaten Gillmore and passed his test.

27

T*uesday*

Tricia flailed. She couldn't catch a breath, like her lungs were hampered by a weight.

She was desperate for air.

Hands pressed her back against a hard surface, as muffled voices issued orders. Something was pushed against her mouth and nose, and a cold stream of air flowed in. An oxygen mask?

"Tricia, you're safe." The strong voice soothed her, cutting through everything else. "Relax and let them take care of you. You're going to be fine." The voice held assurance. It was a promise he would keep.

Tricia relaxed and sank into darkness.

~

HER EYELIDS FLUTTERED. She felt tired, her mind foggy. Tricia forced her eyes open, then closed them against the brightness.

"Wakey, wakey, Beautiful." That could only be Caleb.

"She's not going to respond to you," Mom chided him. "Sweetie, can you open your eyes? Let us know you're okay?"

Tricia sighed. It felt like an effort, but...

A voice cleared. "Please wake up. I need you, Tricia. More than I knew." The pain int that voice forced her to open her eyes. There he was. Her knight in shining armor. The man who had risked his life to save hers.

"Hi."

Caleb chuckled. "Should have known it'd be the firefighter who gets her to cooperate."

"He's better-looking."

Noah shook his head, and ducked his chin.

"Gillmore?"

"In custody." Caleb stared at her as if trying to assure himself she was okay. "We got there as he left. Officers pulled him over within ten minutes. We think Gillmore focused on Noah because, in his mind, Noah and the other firemen were supposed to get him and his son out unharmed."

Tricia felt a rush of certainty. This could be it.

"And you were the attorney who got me off." Noah's look warmed her from the inside out. He smiled in a slow way that stretched out the connection. "Though I didn't want to admit it then."

"And the death of his son freed him to exact revenge," Tricia concluded. Gillmore had lost something irreplaceable when his son died. She remembered what it felt like to lose her father, and could imagine the pain of the reverse. Parents were supposed to die before their children. And those children were not supposed to die from horrible injuries. Yet Timothy had. And his father had watched.

Tricia closed her eyes, weariness sweeping across her. So much had been lost because a man became trapped in his grief.

"Hey, guys. Time to clear out." Noah's voice held a firm tone.

She could imagine him shooing the others out of the room. She peeked, and stifled a laugh as she caught Caleb staring Noah down, then let her eyes close again. They were so heavy.

"Do you need anything before we leave?" Noah's voice was so gentle, she felt drawn to him.

Tricia opened her eyes, and looked into the face of the man who'd risked his life to save hers. She shuddered at the thought of what would have happened if he'd hesitated in his efforts. "Thank you."

He sat next to her as if his legs had collapsed underneath him. "I almost lost you." Noah's voice cracked, and he took her hand. "The thought of losing you like I lost my dad almost paralyzed me. But I had to try."

Words seemed so inadequate. "Thank you." She'd have to say those words innumerable times to convey her gratitude.

"Tricia, I probably shouldn't do this now. I mean, you're lying in a hospital bed." He ran his free hand through his hair. "What I'm trying to say is, Tricia, will you join me for a date this weekend? I was a fool not to ask you a year ago, and I don't want to waste another minute." He stroked her cheek, and her breathing stilled. "Tricia, I've been attracted to you since the first time I saw you. You are a beautiful woman, but now I know that beauty extends all the way to your soul."

She put a finger on his lips and he stopped talking. "Yes, Noah. Get me out of this hospital, and we can go right now."

A chuckle escaped. "Uh-uh. No way am I breaking you out of here. We'll wait until the doctor releases you." His gaze traveled from her eyes to her lips.

Everything in her wanted him to kiss her, but she waited. Just when she thought he'd decided against it, Noah leaned in and kissed her so tenderly she knew he'd hold her heart gently.

Tricia put her arms around his neck and tugged him closer, holding on to the man who treated her like a gift.

~

Two days later, Noah ran through the paperwork with Weary. They'd covered the bases, and Weary could handle the rest of it.

"Good job, Brust. You've got potential if you decide to follow through on investigation." Weary's words made Noah stand up straighter.

"Even though I ran a side investigation?"

"We might have to work on your ability to follow orders, but you showed good instincts. That's the hard part to train into someone." Weary leaned back in his chair, eyes on the fire map on his wall. "I'm glad to check those fires off our list."

Noah nodded. If only they'd worked a little smarter or faster, both on the fires Gillmore had set, and the one that eventually had taken his son from him, starting this whole nightmare.

It sobered Noah how little it took to have a mind slip off the edge of sanity. Gillmore remained convinced that he had exacted justice from those he targeted. Remorse hadn't set in. That would probably develop only in time for the judge and jury to witness. Noah straightened his shoulders. He'd have to watch that he didn't get cynical over this case. Tricia had lost a lot. Her home and possessions. Some of her professional standing. But she hadn't lost her hope.

And hopefully she'd gained him.

Noah glanced at the clock on the wall. Time to get home or he wouldn't pick her up on time. He grinned at the thought of an evening with her. No trial to separate them. No villain to chase. Just the future to explore.

Progress would likely stutter along at first. But it would come.

An hour later he left his apartment, a smile on his face. Jessie was still staying at Dani's home, but she'd come home soon. Then his apartment wouldn't feel so empty.

He eased into his truck and drove to Dani's. Anticipation buzzed through his veins. This was the beginning of a new chapter in his life. One he'd longed for a year ago. He pulled around the corner and parked. His limp had eased, and soon he stood on the front porch, a bouquet of flowers in hand. Noah rang the doorbell and waited.

The sound of heels on the wood floor echoed toward him. A moment later someone fumbled with the door. It swung inward to reveal Tricia.

His breath caught at the sight of her.

Her brown hair glistened and her eyes shone. A light radiated from within. Maybe she felt the same hope for new beginnings. Her shy smile lit up his night. "Hi."

"Ready for dinner?"

She nodded. "We're leaving, Dani."

A muffled answer reached his ears. He offered his arm. "Your chariot awaits."

Her hand felt light on his arm. Their shoulders jostled as they walked down the stairs. Noah pulled Tricia to his side, and she didn't resist.

As they drove toward the restaurant, Noah wished the weather were better, more conducive to a picnic under the stars. Instead, they'd eat at the Green Gateau. Make their own memories there.

Tricia sighed. At the next red light he looked at her. "Everything okay? I mean as much as it can be?"

Her eyes closed, she nodded slightly. "Yes. Everything will come together." She opened her eyes, and their rich cinnamon color caught him by surprise again. "Thank you."

What did she mean? The light turned green and he drove through the intersection. "What?"

"Thank you for tonight."

"We've barely started."

"I know. But I can already tell it will be a wonderful night."

"The first of many?" He glanced over in time to catch her soft smile.

"Yes." Her quiet assurance settled on him.

They'd have their chance at happiness after all, now that the trial by fire had ended.

EPILOGUE

S*ix Months Later*

The sun peeked through the clouds to illuminate the flowering daffodils and crocuses. March's early intensity had abated, leaving a beautiful Saturday for Dani's wedding.

"Are you ready to start this next chapter?"

Tricia dropped the curtain and turned from the window. "You're the one starting a new life."

Dani glowed. "Yes, but I meant staying here. Making this your home."

Tricia looked around the bedroom. She hadn't planned to stay with Dani for six months, but it had been easier to do that while she decided on her next steps. Then Caleb and Dani had decided to sell her place and make their home at his cabin. It had seemed logical to buy the house, one she already loved and whose twin she'd tried to find unsuccessfully. "I think you'll regret moving to the cabin."

"Maybe. But it was important to Caleb and gives us a chance to find the right place for us." Dani ran her fingers along the woodworking. "Much as I love this home, I don't mind leaving the memories of Phil Baker and his stalking behind. Besides, I can come visit you here."

"Newlyweds." Tricia rolled her eyes. "I'm sure that will be your top priority in the coming weeks."

"Not if we don't get to the church."

They bundled up and hurried to Dani's Mustang. Tricia watched her friend bubble with enthusiasm. In some ways this day was years late in coming. At the same time, Tricia wondered if their marriage wouldn't be stronger because of the experiences they'd had and the way Caleb and Dani had rediscovered each other and their love.

"Don't go getting all philosophical and mushy on me."

Tricia smiled. "I didn't say a thing."

"You didn't have to. I could see it in your eyes. Your day is coming."

Even six months ago, Tricia would have fought the idea. But that was before God had stripped the pain of her past...and before Noah started wooing her. Now she could imagine a future shared with a man who challenged her and completed her.

Dani pulled into the church parking lot. "Come on. We've got to hurry."

Laughing, the women pulled bags filled with toiletries and accessories from the trunk. Tricia's mom had brought the dresses earlier.

Tricia had attended services and weddings at Pleasant Hill Community Church for years. The vaulted ceilings and numerous stained-glass windows created a picture-perfect setting for the ceremonies. Today felt different, though. Today her brother would marry her best friend.

The stones in the foyer and hallways had been worn smooth from almost one hundred years of feet treading on them. The click of their shoes echoed off the walls as they hurried to the room where they'd dress. As they walked past, Tricia peeked into the sanctuary.

"Dani, the guys and Logan are already in there."

Dani squealed and picked up her pace. "They'll have to wait."

Tricia and her mom helped Dani into her gown. A beautiful sheath dress, sequins sprinkled along the waist and sleeves in a delicate vine pattern. It fit Dani as if it had been made for her.

Dani's mother swept into the room and beamed. "You look like a dream, darling."

"Thank you." Dani stepped into her shoes, then shooed Tricia. "Hurry up before Caleb thinks I've changed my mind."

Tricia pulled on her emerald tea-length dress, then adjusted the neckline. With the long white gloves and ballet slippers, she felt as if Dani had molded her into Audrey Hepburn's image.

"Quit staring at yourself in the mirror and get over here." Dani tapped her toes against the floor. "I need you to go tell Caleb to close his eyes. And remind Logan that he needs to photograph Caleb when he sees me. I want to capture his expression."

Tricia slipped from the room and into the sanctuary. "You guys ready for Dani?"

Caleb fidgeted with his jacket sleeves, a sheen of perspiration on his forehead. "Does she know she's late?"

"It's worth it. I promise. But keep your eyes closed until it's time for Dani to walk down the aisle. She wants a picture of your expression. Are you ready, Logan?"

Logan hefted his camera and grinned. "We'll be in position."

She tilted her chin and glanced at Noah. His stare stopped the coquettish expression she tried to convey. He looked at her in a way that said it didn't matter what Dani or anyone else looked like: he only had eyes for her. Her breath caught at the love expressed so freely and openly in his gaze.

He had been such a gift to her. One straight from the Heavenly Father. That God could connect her with a man who didn't see her past but saw her future...the thought humbled her on an almost daily basis.

Caleb cleared his throat, and Tricia tore her gaze from Noah's.

"I'll go get Dani now."

"Thanks."

In a few minutes, Pachelbel's *Canon in D* wafted from the sound system. Tricia straightened Dani's train, then prepared to walk down the aisle.

Noah turned from his seat in the second row to watch her. There was a promise in his gaze.

A promise she couldn't wait to explore.

DEADLY EXPOSURE

Chapter One

Dani Richards barely noticed where the usher pointed as she turned to take Aunt Jayne's arm but groped emptiness. Dani spun in a circle, searching for her. "Aunt Jayne?"

"She went that way, ma'am."

Dani nodded at the usher and hurried across the plush red carpet toward the boxes. She slipped into their box, but it remained empty. Then she heard a raised voice from the adjoining box. She darted to it, parted the curtain and pushed through. Aunt Jayne relaxed next to a young woman whose stiff back and chin pointed high made it clear she was trying to avoid eye contact. "There you are. You scared me to death, Aunt Jayne."

"No need to worry. I looked for our seats and found this lovely young lady instead."

"You don't belong here." The woman looked from Dani to her aunt, emerald eyes flashing. Her regal bearing sagged with a hint of disappointment. She glanced beyond Dani into the emptying foyer.

Aunt Jayne patted her hand. "Don't worry. Your young man will join you. You're too lovely to miss."

Dani examined the woman more closely, wondering why she seemed so familiar. In her job as a reporter, she worked with too many people to count in an average week, but this woman tugged at her memory. "Have we met before?"

"Please leave." With a quick twist of her wrist the woman glanced at her watch.

"Sorry for the interruption. Come on, Aunt Jayne. *Cats* starts any minute." Together they reentered the foyer and slipped up the stairs to the right box. Dani released a deep breath, determined to enjoy every moment of the evening. After the latest trial she'd covered on her crime beat for Channel 17, she'd earned the reprieve. Her aunt deserved her full attention on a night when the cloud of Alzheimer's had slipped away, even fleetingly.

Aunt Jayne sank into her seat and smiled. "Thank you for bringing me, dear. It's so nice to have you in town again."

Dani settled beside her in a maroon seat as the orchestra crescendoed into the opening notes of the musical, prepared to relish each moment. She'd spent the five years since graduation working her way through the ranks of broadcast journalism, moving from Cheyenne to Des Moines to St. Louis. She'd given it all up to move to Lincoln for Aunt Jayne. Her mom believed she'd lost her mind, and her dad tried to convince her to take a job at his station in Chicago each time they talked.

Lincoln had been lonely, especially when Aunt Jayne's bad days outnumbered the good. She'd wanted to dance when she reached Peaceful Estates and found Aunt Jayne alert and excited. A sliver remained of the woman Dani remembered from summers spent in Lincoln. If only she reappeared more often.

The curtain rose, and Dani leaned into the railing. She glanced at the neighboring box, but couldn't see more than outlines in the darkness. The opening song began, and her attention focused completely on the stage covered by a large set that resembled a junkyard. The actors stretched and danced as they mimicked cats and sang. The scenes flew by, and too soon the curtain sank for intermission.

Dani shifted against the seat and straightened. Renee Thomas. That was the woman's name. She'd interviewed the grad student for a story on promising research at the university. Though Renee had been formal and distant tonight, she'd been much friendlier and relaxed during the interview. Odd, since people tended to freeze in that setting. She'd practically glowed as she discussed the research, something about protecting the food supply from terrorist attacks. Dani had worked with her to describe the research in layman's terms.

Aunt Jayne tapped Dani's arm lightly. Dani smiled. "Are you okay? Need a break from sitting?"

"Maybe we should hunt for the story. Surely it's hiding somewhere." Aunt Jayne looked at her, amusement glowing in her eyes.

"There's a loose plot, keep watch." Dani stretched in her seat and her gaze slid into the box to her right. Renee sat motionless. She studied the woman, remembering the edge of worry that marred her expression. Renee had remained alone after all. "Let's stretch our legs a bit."

They stepped into the wide hallway. Dani looked around, hoping tonight wouldn't be the time she ran into the only person she'd allowed to break her heart. Caleb Jamison. The thought of him made her emotions spiral into a tornado of anger and hurt. She looked over her shoulder, afraid he'd appear like some horror-movie ghoul. Wished she could wipe her memory of him.

"Aunt Jayne, let's step up here. I interviewed your new friend last week. Maybe she'd like to join us."

Dani approached the neighboring box. She knocked on the doorframe, parted the curtain and entered the woman's box. A spicy fragrance tinged the air.

"Renee?" Dani waited a moment. The woman never turned. The seconds ticked by. "Are you enjoying the show? Andrew Lloyd Webber is a genius."

Renee remained silent. Dani stepped closer. One part of her mind began to insist she leave. Now.

Dani tapped Renee on the shoulder. Her skin felt cool. With

quick steps she circled the seat and stood in front of Renee. Dani looked down, looking for a flash of recognition. Instead, Renee's gaze remained fixed, a horrible grimace pasted to her face. The emerald scarf wound tight around her neck in contrast to the way it floated earlier.

She sucked in a breath and willed herself to remain calm. Between the tightness of the scarf and the bruise lying under the woman's jaw, Dani's instinct jumped to murder. Bile rose in her throat. She put a hand over her mouth and swallowed.

This couldn't be happening again. Images of her college roommate's distorted features floated in front of Renee's. She'd been too late then. She couldn't be now. Dani rushed into the hall, fumbled for the cell phone in her evening bag and dialed 911. No service. She thrust the phone back into her purse. "Somebody call 911. There's a medical emergency. Does anyone know CPR?"

She didn't wait for an answer but ran back into the box. She sensed someone behind her. and turned to find Aunt Jayne. She pulled her attention back to Renee, and tried to ease her to the floor, struggling under the leaden weight.

Please don't let it be too late.

Concerned faces peered into Dani's from around the curtain. A well-dressed gentleman slipped into the box. He eased Renee the rest of the way to the floor, then loosened the scarf. He checked the woman's neck for a pulse. Dani watched him silently tick the seconds off his watch for an eternal moment. He shook his head and glanced at her. "It's too late."

Dani shuddered. She rose to her feet and took Aunt Jayne by the arm. "Let's get you back to our seats where you can be comfortable." A couple minutes later, Dani stood in the foyer. She took a step toward Renee's box, then turned back to her own. Aunt Jayne seemed fine, but Dani hesitated.

The news director would expect a complete report. She'd found the body, so she'd own the story from this moment. Somehow she'd balance that with caring for Aunt Jayne until she was back in her suite at Peaceful Estates. Interview questions ran through her mind. Someone had to have seen something.

"Ma'am, you have to stay until the police arrive." A tenor voice tickled her ear.

Dani jumped back against the wall. She turned toward the sound. An usher had invaded her space and her gaze met a fishy stare.

"You're a reporter with Channel 17, right?" He slid a half step back and licked his lips. "They...the police, I mean, should be here soon. They'll want to talk to you. You found the body."

She stepped to the side, unable to bear his proximity. "I promise I won't leave before the police arrive."

"Maybe I should clear the box." His gaze darted around the small area.

"It's a little late for that. Quite a few people have moved in and out already."

"Still, there must be something. They never told us what to do in a situation like this." Beads of sweat pooled on his brow as he twisted the top button of his shirt open. Angry uncertainty flashed across his face.

Dani leaned farther into the wall. "Are you okay? I'd be happy to get help."

"I'm fine." With a parting glare and tug at his collar, he turned on his heel and headed down the hall.

Dani watched him disappear, and then turned to the box. A security guard huffed up the stairs. A couple followed him. The man, tall and trim with a long stride, caught her eye. The woman held his arm and managed to keep up without looking rushed. Every brown piece of hair was in place, and her blue cocktail dress perfectly fit her athletic form. The man looked at her. Dani froze. One look in Caleb Jamison's face, and she reverted to the teenager head over heels for the star football player. The teenager who couldn't say no. The teenager who ached when he stopped seeing her. Stopped calling. Stopped caring.

The ice disappeared in a flash of anger. Her hands trembled. Her stomach clenched at the thought of his smug, self-satisfied face. She couldn't go back there. The echo of their baby's cries as she was given to others jarred Dani's mind. Caleb had abandoned her long before the birth. Yet here he was, cocky smile and all. He took a step toward her, and Dani escaped into the box.

Intrigued? Want to read the rest of Dani's story in Deadly Exposure? *Then go to your favorite bookstore or online retailer to purchase it.*

DEAR READER,

Thank you so much for joining me in Tricia and Noah's story. I hope you enjoyed the return of Caleb and Dani as well.

This book was fun to write, as I returned to suspense. I loved watching the librarians' expressions as I checked out books and videos on arson, fires and other suspense topics. Sometimes I could see the questions they wanted to ask, but didn't. It was also a lot of fun to pull in some of my trial experience, as Tricia fought her courtroom battles.

Domestic violence is an all-too-real problem. I've seen lives and families damaged and destroyed by the violence that occurs in a place that should be safest of all: the family. So I understand Tricia's passion for protecting those who can't stand on their own.

Tricia and Noah are both stripped of things that matter to them. Tricia sacrifices some of her reputation and many of her possessions; Noah wrestles with a chronic injury. And both wrestle with having their weaknesses and secrets exposed. Tricia, in particular, struggles with how to respond in a way that honors God.

As the prophet Micah says, God requires us to act justly and show mercy. Tricia grapples with this, longing to wrap bitterness and anger around her, but knowing that she can't. That God demands more of her. What a lesson for each of us. To chase after justice and mercy. To live lives that honor God in this pursuit.

I hope you enjoyed this journey!

QUESTIONS FOR DISCUSSION

1. Tricia hides a large part of her past from others, even those closest to her. How does this hurt her?
2. Does ignoring the past ever help the one who's been hurt? Why or why not?
3. If you could have coffee with Tricia, how would you encourage her to release the pain of her past? How has God helped you do the same thing in your life?
4. How has God been able to use the painful experiences of your life to strengthen you and your walk with Him?
5. Have you ever felt abandoned by God or your family? How did you resolve that feeling of abandonment?
6. Noah is a guys' guy, into the active lifestyle before he's injured on the job. How does he cope with the changes imposed on him by his chronic pain?
7. Taking on new responsibilities can be a challenge. How does Noah deal with the new challenges in his role as a fledgling fire investigator?
8. If you could counsel Noah, how would you suggest that he handle Weary?
9. Opening up to love requires vulnerability. How does Tricia

reach a point that she can open herself to love? Noah and Tricia begin a relationship by risking and trusting. What benefits have you experienced from taking similar risks?

10. Tricia is blindsided in court and all her secrets are exposed. What process does this begin in her life? How does God use this event?
11. Tricia loses everything material. Have you had to start over? What was the experience like?

ABOUT THE AUTHOR

Cara C. Putman, JD MBA, the award-winning author of 35 books, graduated high school at 16, college at 20, and completed her law degree at 27. FIRST for Women magazine called Shadowed by Grace "captivating" and a "novel with 'the works.'" Beyond Justice is being called a page-turner that can't be put down.

Cara is active at her church and a full-time lecturer on business and employment law to graduate students at Purdue University's Krannert School of Management. Putman also practices law and is a second-generation homeschooling mom. She serves on the executive board of American Christian Fiction Writers (ACFW), an organization she has served in various roles since 2007. She lives with her husband and four children in Indiana.

Connect with Cara and read first chapters of her books on her website: Http://caraputman.com/books.

ALSO BY CARA C. PUTMAN

WWII Historical Romances

Canteen Dreams

Captive Dreams

A Promise Forged

A Promise Born

A Promise Kept

Cornhusker Dreams

Buckeye Promises

WWII Romantic Mysteries

Shadowed by Grace

Stars in the Night

Legal Thrillers

Beyond Justice

Imperfect Justice

Delayed Justice

Flight Risk

Lethal Intent

Romantic Suspense

Deadly Secrets on Mackinac Island

Dying for Love, novella prequel to *Beyond Justice*

Hidden Love, novella

Deadly Exposure, book 1 in Hometown Heroes

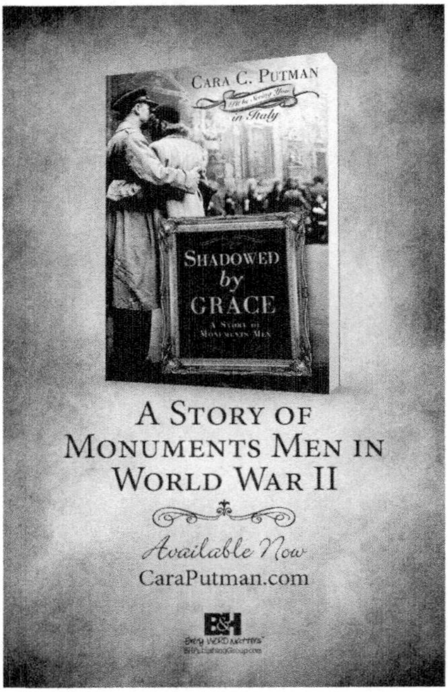
CARA C. PUTMAN
in Italy
SHADOWED by GRACE
A STORY OF MONUMENTS MEN
A STORY OF MONUMENTS MEN IN WORLD WAR II
Available Now
CaraPutman.com
B&H

BEYOND JUSTICE EXCERPT

PROLOGUE

JANUARY

If he didn't find that flash drive now, he would have to disappear.

Immediately.

Some place el jefe couldn't find him. It was that or die.

"Where is it, Miguel? What have you done with the information you stole?"

The young man shuddered as he choked on a breath. Blood poured from his nose, broken in the first punch, the horror of it fresh. Blood dribbled out his mouth. Blood dripped off his chin. Still he refused to speak.

Rafael drew back his fist, ready to strike again, then held his arm back as if against a powerful force. This was not who he was. It was not who Miguel was. All of this was so broken. Somehow he had landed on the wrong side of the great family his own had served for three generations.

How was he now opposing the young man he loved like a brother? He scanned the bare room. Four bunk beds lined a wall. A urinal in the corner. A barren sink with a square mirror. A single light bulb hanging well above his head. Where could Miguel have hidden anything in this desolate place?

The stench of urine and sweat, of bodies crammed into a space designed for half as many, mixed with the coppery aroma of fresh blood.

Limp sunlight pushed back the shadows from a barred window high on the wall. Sunlight that reminded him of the times Miguel had tagged along when Rafael did odd chores at the estate. Sunlight that reminded him how wrong it was for Miguel to be here. He was the son of a lord, not someone who should be locked up.

"Where is it, Miguel? I can't ask again." He flipped open the blade of the knife he held and slid it under Miguel's chin. "Give it to me, or I have no choice but to kill you."

Miguel flinched. "We always have a choice." The youth lifted his chin and met Rafael's gaze with pain-filled eyes. "We are brothers, Rafael."

"We were. If you don't give me that flash drive, we are both dead."

"I don't know what you're talking about."

"Liar! El jefe knows you were in his computer. He told me himself. He sent me."

"You kill me, and my father will hunt you like a rabid mongrel." False bravado flashed in Miguel's eyes.

"Your father told me to kill you, amigo."

The spoken words resounded in the narrow space between them. He looked at señor's precious son. His heir. Could he somehow take Miguel with him and disappear? No. Would Miguel give him the list? The boy raised dark eyes to meet his gaze, defiance hardening them. Somehow Rafael had imagined he could avoid killing while serving the family even as he'd crept up its structure. But now he had no choice.

Retrieve the information for el jefe before it falls into the wrong hands or be killed.

Heat flooded him and red clouded his vision.

"I'm sorry, Miguel . . ." He stepped forward, knife clasped in his fist.

CHAPTER ONE

THURSDAY, MARCH 30

The euphoria of winning a hard case vied in her thoughts with wondering what came next as Hayden McCarthy left the Alexandria courthouse. A colorful dance of tulips lined a flower box of the town house across the street, and the faint aroma of some hidden blossom scented the air. It was over.

Her client had needed her absolute best. Hayden had delivered it and obtained justice. She shifted her purse and readjusted her briefcase as she started down the street. Continue straight on King Street, and in a block she'd be at the office. Turn, and in four blocks she'd be home. Her town house's proximity both to work and the heart of Old Town Alexandria was why she loved the space she shared with a friend from law school.

So . . . which way to go? The thought of going back to her office and confronting the waiting pile of work held no appeal. She would spend one night savoring success . . . and recovering from the adrenaline pace of a roller-coaster trial and jury.

She'd make a salad and cup of tea, maybe pick up a novel. If that didn't hold her attention, she'd dig into her trial notes. Analyze what had worked and how the risk of requesting a new foreman after deliberations had begun had paid off.

Each step closer to home, her conservative navy pumps tapped the refrain. She. Had. Won. She let a smile spread across her face.

She left King Street and headed north on St. Asaph. Some of the buildings she passed housed businesses, but with each block the area became more residential. In one condo a senator lived. In another a congressman, next to him a chief of staff and other people with powerful political positions. When Hayden first moved to the city from small-town Nebraska, her head had turned at how easy it was to rub elbows with those who controlled destinities. Now it was only scandals or surprise retirements that caught her attention.

The evening was so pleasant she detoured and walked the couple blocks to Christ Church. The wrought iron fence around the church grounds beckoned her to settle in the shade of the stately trees. She opened the gate, then walked until she reached a bench. Settling on it, she breathed deeply and closed her eyes.

Father, thank You. It went well today. She pushed against her eyes, daring relieved tears to fall. There was no one else around, and Hayden sat quietly, waiting . . . for something. Here within the shelter of a church more than two hundred years old, shouldn't she feel God's presence?

Yet there was . . . nothing.

Not even a rustle of a breeze through the leaves that she could pretend was the Spirit moving.

I need You.

Still nothing. Then slowly she sensed His smile as warmth spread through her.

A couple came around the corner then, strolling along the garden path arm in arm, smiling at one another. They looked at ease and in tune as their strides matched.

What would it feel like to be that comfortable and safe with someone? To know you could trust another person with your most hidden parts? Hayden shook her head. Her life was full to the brim—no room for a relationship. She stood and walked the rest of the way home at a brisk pace.

When she reached her town house, she crossed the courtyard and dug her keys loose from the pit of her purse. The Wonder Woman keyring, a gift from a grateful client after she won what he called the unwinnable case, jiggled as she unlocked the door.

The moment she walked inside, Hayden kicked off her heels and set her bag on the chair next to the glass table by the door. Soft classical music flowed from the kitchen, and the aroma of something spicy filled the small space.

"Emilie?" Hayden leaned down to rub one of her arches, then straightened and moved toward the kitchen.

"Down here." Emilie Wesley's bubbly voice came from the stairway leading to the basement. "Can you check the oven for me?"

"Sure. What are you making?" Hayden moved around the granite countertop and turned on the oven light. Emilie was a wonderful cook, but she often got distracted. "Mmm, lasagna. Looks great. It's bubbling around the edges, and the cheese looks perfect. You expecting company?"

Hayden opened the fridge and pulled out salad ingredients. A salad plus a glass of sweet tea and she could disappear into her room . . .though the pasta looked wonderful. If she was lucky, Emilie would save her some for lunch tomorrow.

Hayden was dicing a red pepper when two sets of footsteps echoed up the stairs.

"Look who stopped by, Hayden."

"Hmm?" Hayden looked up and into clear blue eyes that matched the Potomac as it moved into the bay. His pressed khakis and Oxford with pullover sweater portrayed an understated GQ elegance that screamed old money and matched the clean haircut and polite smile that revealed teeth so perfect they might be caps. Andrew Wesley, her roommate's cousin. She hadn't seen him in years.

The knife slipped, and she felt a sharp pain in her finger. She turned on the tap and stuck her finger beneath the flow of cold water.

"Andrew, do you remember my roommate, Hayden McCarthy? Hayden, this is my cousin Andrew. It's been a while, but I'm pretty sure y'all have met before." Emilie's eyes danced as she tugged the man into the room. His mouth curved into a relaxed grin, the look as familiar and practiced as Hayden's in court.

The years had been good to Andrew Wesley. He'd been handsome when they'd first met, but now he was something more. He had the build of someone who worked out and took care of himself. Compact, muscular, and distractingly good-looking. Hayden pasted a smile into place.

"Hayden?" The deep voice was thick as the richest chocolate. "It's nice to officially meet you—again." He gave her a devastating smile.

"Emilie is always talking about you."

"Good things, I hope." She grabbed a paper towel and turned off the water.

"What else would I say?" Emilie's eyes widened as she saw blood seeping through the paper towel. "Ooh, do you need a Band-Aid?"

"I'll be all right." Hayden took a deep breath and met Andrew's gaze.

"Any friend—or cousin—of Emilie's is welcome here." With her good hand she scooped up the diced pepper and sprinkled it on top of the salad. "I'll leave you two to enjoy your dinner. It looks good, Em."

"You don't need to leave, Hayden." Emilie leaned closer, not hard to do in the galley space that felt even smaller with Andrew's presence, and handed Hayden a fresh paper towel. "We're working on plans for a spring festival. Think inflatables, fair food, and fun. It's a community event for his non-profit." She grabbed a purple grape from a bowl next to the sink and popped it into her mouth. "You can help us."

His cousin's roommate wrapped the paper towel tighter around her finger, then turned to the refrigerator, shielding her face from his view.

Had they really met before? He had a vague recollection of an awkward girl visiting his cousin during a law school break, but his memory didn't match this attractive woman with the black hair and . . . stocking feet.

As Hayden put away the vegetables she'd used for her salad, Andrew looked for something to break the uncomfortable silence.

"I like the idea of a festival, Em, but I'm not sure we can pull it off."

"Oh? You already have the location." Emilie claimed the pot holders and opened the oven. "We can do this because we're the dynamic duo. Besides, you've got a staff and board of directors to help. We'll create the framework, and they can do the rest."

Andrew shook his head. "You haven't worked much with a board. And don't forget, I'm not the senior guy in the office."

Emilie slid the pan from the oven and set it on top of the stove.

"You're a Wesley. Everyone takes one look at you and snaps to attention. Your dad is too powerful to tick off." She softened the words with a smile. "You might as well embrace it."

That was something that hadn't happened yet in his thirty years. Being Scott Wesley's son was like wearing a coat made for someone else.

He leaned against the counter and redirected the conversation—a skill he'd picked up from his father. "I've heard about Emilie's day, Hayden. Tell me about yours."

Hayden paused, salad dressing in hand. "I won a case today."

"Oh?" He studied her face, but she didn't give anything away. Not much of a talker?

She shrugged. "I kept an innocent man out of jail. So it was a great day for my client and his wife."

"For you too." Emilie stepped next to Hayden and squeezed her shoulder. "This woman worked a lot of late nights on that case and is on the fast track to becoming a partner." Hayden started to protest, but Emilie kept on. "She'll never brag about herself, but she's good. Nobody will be surprised when she becomes the youngest partner in Elliott & Johnson history."

Soft color tinted the woman's cheeks, and she glanced at Andrew. "I'm not any better than a hundred other attorneys in town."

Only a hundred, huh? In a city overwhelmed with attorneys, she'd ranked herself fairly high. Well, the last thing he wanted to do was spend free time with an attorney. He'd spent too much time in their presence growing up to be wowed by their brilliance or awed by their stories.

She held up her salad bowl and fork. "I know y'all have plans to make, so I'll slip upstairs and not interrupt. It was nice to see you again, Andrew."

Andrew put a hand on her arm before she could disappear. "You really want to walk away from Emilie's lasagna for that?" He crinkled his nose and pointed at the bowl of greens.

Emilie grabbed an extra plate. "There's plenty, Hayden."

Andrew grinned. "Always is. She forgets there's only two of us."

He said it as though these evenings were frequent, but they weren't.

Emilie was as busy as anyone in town, so he'd pounced on her invitation. When they all sat down at the island a few minutes later, he watched Hayden. She looked tired. A good trial would do that, his dad always said. He and Emilie kept a quiet conversation going, with Hayden interjecting now and then.

She'd made it through law school, and he admired anyone who did that. He'd quit after a semester—but that had more to do with wanting to become his own man rather than an ever-lengthening part of his father's shadow.

A phone beeped, and Hayden glanced at hers and frowned. "Sorry, but I need to prepare for a meeting in the morning. Nice to see you, Andrew." She stood and brushed past him with a small smile.

He watched her cross the living space and head toward the stairs. As she climbed from view he reminded himself that he didn't have time to feel attracted to anyone right now. Not when Congressman Wesley was gunning for a title change. Anyone he was seen with would end up plastered across the social pages of the Post the next day. Who would willingly sign up for that?

He turned back to the kitchen and found Emilie smirking at him.

"I'm not sure you're her type, Andrew." Her smile widened until her dimples showed.

He made a face at her. "Don't think I don't see right through you. I know why you had me meet you here." He was just surprised it had taken this long. "It doesn't matter. I'm too busy to get involved right now."

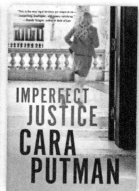

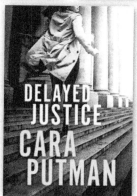

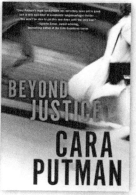